BRINLIN
ISLE

BOOKS BY ROBIN STEPHEN

Chronicles of the Tessilari
Tessili Academy
Tessili Rogue
Tessili Revenge

Annals of the Brinlocks
Brinlin Isle
Brinlin Forest
Brinlin Cove

Brinlin Isle

Annals of the Brinlocks: Book I

A Story of Bydaira

Robin Stephen

This is a work of fiction. All characters, events, and organization portrayed in this novel are either product's of the author's imagination or are used fictitiously.

BRINLIN ISLE

Copyright © 2017 by Brown Wing Press

robinstephen.com

ISBN 978-1-946238-00-9 (ebook)
ISBN 978-1-946238-03-0 (print)

Cover design by Robin Deutschendorf
Maps by Robin Deutschendorf

Brown Wing Press
Iowa City, IA
brownwingpress.com

First Brown Wing Press Edition

This little series is dedicated to the wonderful teachers I had in 3rd, 4th, 5th, and 6th grade who went out of their way to show an interest in my youthful scribblings. It's impossible to overstate the vast impact so much early support and valuable feedback had on my desire to keep writing, and get better at it.

ELYS YINS

CARREG DINAS

GOL LEDRITH

NELYNA
(FOG ISLES)

LAN DINAS

TWO TRIALS

SERPEN

SHR

N

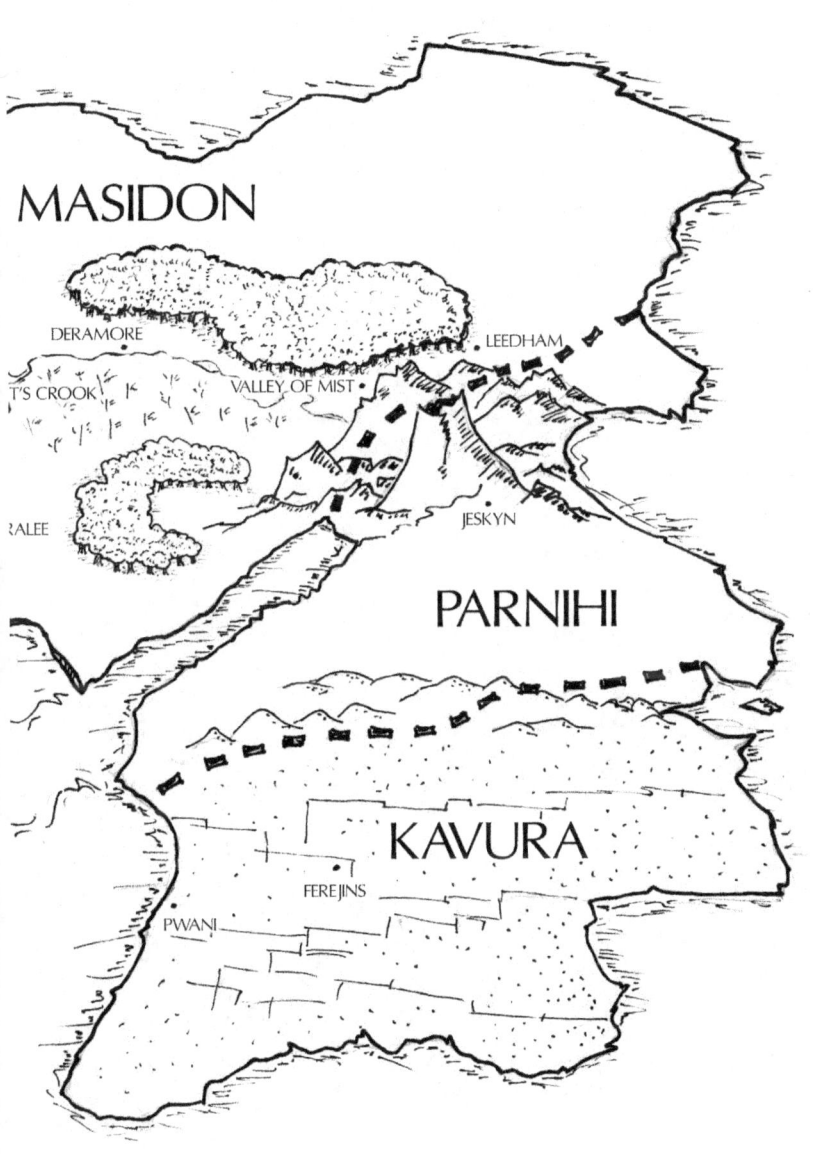

BYDAIRA

MASIDON

DERAMORE

T'S CROOK

VALLEY OF MIST

LEEDHAM

RALEE

JESKYN

PARNIHI

KAVURA

FEREJINS

PWANI

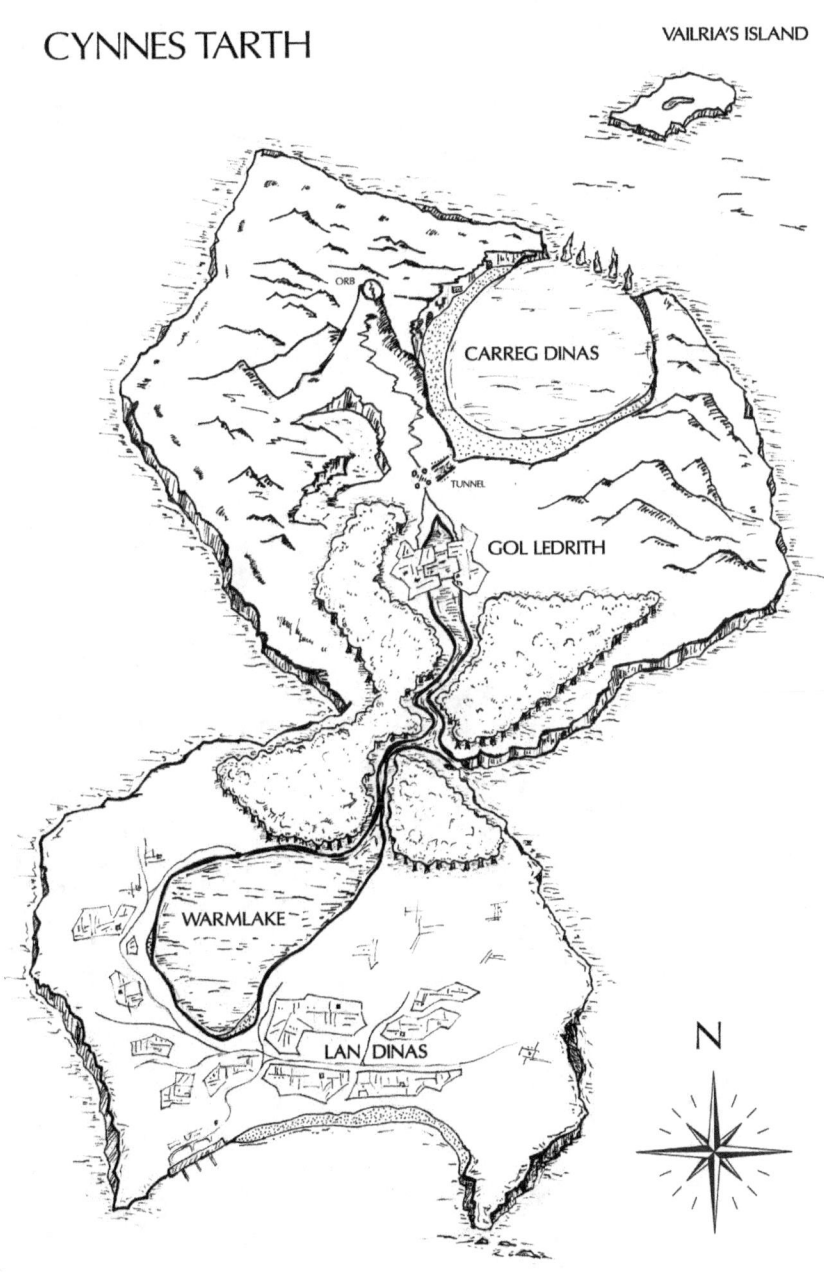

CYNNES TARTH

VAILRIA'S ISLAND

ORB

CARREG DINAS

TUNNEL

GOL LEDRITH

WARMLAKE

LAN DINAS

N

PRELUDE

The fog was alive and thrumming with dark energy. As lightning snaked and danced in the sky overhead, the fog coiled and looped like the flight path of a maddened tessila.

Marim knelt on the narrow path that led from Lan Dinas down to the shores of the warmlake, staring ahead into the gray air. She could taste the fog—its rusty tang—but couldn't see more than a few feet in any direction. It was like being utterly alone on her own private, half-made planet.

She could feel the creeping coolness as her skirts soaked up the pooling dew and mud. She blinked and rubbed her eyes, but it didn't help. The fog muffled everything. She blinked again, swaying.

Marim was tired, and growing cold. The wind blowing ahead of the storm traced probing fingers up the nape of her neck. She shivered, her nostrils full of the scent of damp, cool earth.

Kix was upset. She could feel him flying above her, wheeling and circling in aimless loops. It was often this way for her tessila.

Strong emotion overwhelmed him, made him directionless and incapable of focusing. Confused by her exhaustion, he flung himself about in the empty sky in an orgy of purposeless activity.

Marim should get up. It was strange of her to be kneeling in the path like this as the storm drew near. Nothing was finished yet. Her help might be needed. Time was running out.

Strangely, though, Marim could not get up. Her limbs felt heavy, as if they'd been poured full of wet sand. Even her heartbeat felt sluggish, as if her blood had grown thick as oil. But next to the slowness, a sense of urgency beat through her like the throbbing rumble of a distant drum.

She must get up.

Marim did not move. It felt like she'd been kneeling on this damp path most of her life. She could hear nothing but the strange hiss of the fog, see nothing but the roiling gray mists. She was having trouble remembering how she'd come to be in this place. Not just on the path, but in this fog-filled world. Her memory was as fuzzy as the blank air.

"Lan Dinas. Cynnes Tarth." She spoke the words aloud, startling herself. The names, she felt, should hold some significance. As it was, they existed like she did – cut off from everything that might give them meaning.

Kix wheeled ever higher in the thick air. Marim drooped. She didn't have to stay sitting, she realized. She could lie down and let her head nestle into the soft grass. She could uncurl her legs and stretch out and rest. She would. In a moment, she would.

She heard the thump of a boot on grass. She looked up to see a shape looming over her. She caught the scent of hair oil and boot leather, saw a pinprick of gleaming gold against a neck scarf.

A thought leapt into her head. *He's come back. He's come back, and he's going to kill me.* The certainty uncoiled from the secret place in her heart where the fear and anger had ridden since that terrible day, long ago, when she'd run into the forest, chased by the sound of screams.

She *must* get up.

She had run away that time. She needed to do it again. Then, she'd been hungry and weak and terrified. Now, there was something wrong in her mind. She was confused, not remembering properly, and Kix was so high up there, flying on the looping currents of wind she could not see.

Marim didn't move. The man loomed. Hands closed around her throat. Tight, rough hands that squeezed with precise, deliberate pressure. She had the absurd thought that at least, with his hands around her throat, he would not be able to see her scars.

The world, already gray, began to go dark around the edges.

CHAPTER 1

The fog clung to the lines and rigging of the tidy merchant vessel, muffling the snap of the sails. It was a damp, restless haze with chilly fingers that crept in at collars and cuffs. It seemed to be growing thicker by the minute, blotting out sight and sound alike.

Marim stood on the deck, hands resting on the rail, staring into the gray air. She could hear the restless waves churning against the prow and feel the rolling of the deck beneath her feet. Over the last two months, she'd grown accustomed to the sounds and sensations of being at sea. She'd also grown used to the view. She'd been staring at the distant horizon for days, that brilliant line where blue sky met blue ocean. Now, she could see only a short distance beyond the rail.

As she strained into the fog, shapes loomed. A man on deck gave a cry. There was an answering call and a thump, then the ship began to bustle with activity. Marim moved off the rail and stood snugged up against a storage crate. She'd been told early on this was a spot she could occupy without getting in the way.

More shapes materialized on the dim air. A smaller vessel appeared down below, ready to guide them into the harbor. Ropes were thrown, men climbed over the rail. Behind her, Marim heard laughter and conversation.

Her heart, already heavy, grew leaden.

"I guess we're here." Marim spoke the words under her breath, but Kix couldn't hear. He was on the other side of the stitchring she wore on its thin chain about her neck. Which meant he was miles upon miles away in the sunny gardens of Tessili Academy, dozing on his brillbane bush.

Not that her tessila would have been any comfort if he had been with her. Kix was erratic, even by tessila standards. Marim's relationship with him was volatile at the best of times. Still, whenever she grew scared or lonely or uncertain, she reflexively wished for his presence.

There was more laughter in the dim mist and a resounding thud and shudder as the ship snugged up to a pier. A smell of overripe fish rose on the briny air, thick and cloying. In no time at all, the vessel was made fast, a gangplank was run out. They had landed in Cynnes Tarth at last.

Marim's journey was over. It was time to go.

Still, she stood by the crate. She knew she should return to the closet-like cabin she'd been assigned when everyone had thought she was going to become a permanent member of the crew. She should sling the ridiculous sea bag she'd traded her trunk for over her shoulder. She should go ashore.

But she couldn't. Marim felt stuck. It was as if her feet were nailed to the deck as surely as the furniture in the captain's cabin. She no longer wanted to be on the ship. The events that had unfolded over the last three weeks had been deeply unpleasant. Had she been a different girl, with a different history, they would have been the most unpleasant of her life. But Marim had lived through far worse.

Still, she also did not want to go ashore and face this place.

Trying to stir herself to action, Marim ran a hand through her damp hair. It was short – short enough it wouldn't fall into her eyes. It was an unfashionable cut. She'd had to argue with the barber to get him to do what she asked. When he'd given in at last, she'd felt a heady thrill at the cold touch of the shears as they snipped along at the base of her neck. Her long, dull hair had fallen to the floor. She'd felt reborn.

She'd been excited then, full of misguided hopes and expectations. This journey had been meant to redeem her, to set her on a new path.

It hadn't worked out at all the way she'd planned.

There was the ringing tramp of booted feet approaching. Captain Tommin's burly outline approached, made pale by the fog. He was a kind man. Ever since the night everything had gone so wrong, he'd assumed an apologetic air when he spoke to Marim, as if what had happened was his fault.

He stopped well away from her. None of the men came within several feet anymore. He cleared his throat and spoke in an overly hearty tone. "We're ready to take you ashore, young miss."

And abandon me to my fate, Marim added silently. Her heart skittered with anxiety. Panic swelled within her. *They're really going to do it*, she thought. *They're going to leave me behind.*

For a moment, Marim felt the old helpless rage. It bloomed through her like poison, filling her blood with heat, making her vision go red at the edges. She felt Kix stir, coming out of his doze. She needed to get ahold of herself, or he'd come blasting through the stitchring and make everything worse.

With an effort, Marim contained her emotions. She forced her face into a smile. "Thank you, captain. I'll go and get my things."

The smell in the butcher's shop had always made Embriem queasy. When he'd been a boy, he always tried to wheedle his way out of errands that involved coming here, often with success.

Then, for a time, he all but forgot about this place. During the days of his brief, happy marriage, his wife, Chalsia, had cheerfully taken over the responsibility of fetching the household meat. But now Chalsia was gone, and Embriem was no longer a boy with indulgent parents who would allow him to worm his way out of what needed to be done.

So he stood at the counter, keeping his breath shallow and trying not to let his discomfort show on his face. His eyes settled on the hanging loops of sausages arranged in tidy rows along the ceiling. He pointed. "And a string of those." He tried to keep his tone casual.

The butcher's boy, Tobb, gaped for a moment, staring at the already formidable pile of wrapped meat on the counter.

Embriem waited, fixing his face in a bland expression and resisting the impulse to offer some explanation. It would be easy. "I'm having a party," or "I'm shopping for my parents as well as myself," would be simple explanations. But they would be lies. And lies, Embriem had learned, always caught up with you in one way or another.

So he stood in patient silence as the boy scrambled around behind the counter, unhooking a string of sausages and coiling them up so he could wrap them in paper. He set the package on the counter with the other lumpy shapes and spoke in a hesitant tone. "Will that be all then?"

The butcher's shop was a tidy place with a sanded counter and large, clean windows to let in whatever sun could make it through the fog. Embriem looked at the other cuts on offer, but he supposed this had to be all. He should have brought a basket. Or his old pack. He could only imagine how the boy would gawk if he loaded all that meat into the worn leather bag he used to carry with him when he spent his days tending his family's herd of goras. The thought was so ridiculous, he almost began to smile.

But the smile stopped as soon as it began. As it always did when his mood lightened a fraction, Embriem's grief came roaring back like an angry bull guarding its herd, charging into his chest to trample on his heart, to remind him he was a terrible man to even think about smiling after what had happened to Chalsia.

The desire to smile died. He considered the meat. How long would it last? A day? Less? He had no way of knowing. "Yes, that's all." His voice sounded gruff and harsh. It made the boy twitch, as if Embriem had struck him.

"I think I'd better go get the master." Tobb was still staring at the mound of packages. "I'm not sure I can calculate it all proper, you know. For the price."

Embriem closed his eyes in a slow blink. He knew rumors would fly, were already flying, about his strange new shopping habits. Whether or not the butcher saw his pile of purchases would make little difference as to who eventually found out about this. Still, the thought of having to see the man's reaction was exhausting. Embriem had to resist the urge to turn on his heel and leave the shop. He wanted to abandon the smell of this place, to leave his pile of meat on the counter and go home.

But he couldn't do that, of course.

Embriem reached into the soft leather purse that hung on his belt and drew out a copper sliver. "Speak with your master," he said. "Bring me the final tally and the meat both within the hour. This is for you, for helping. All right?"

The thin coin gave a click as Embriem set it on the smooth counter. The boy blinked several times in rapid succession. Embriem didn't give him time to argue. Doubtless, the lad was needed here in the shop. Doubtless, Embriem could have taken the meat and settled up with the butcher later. He'd known the man his entire life. Everyone knew Embriem had come from one of the wealthiest families on Cynnes Tarth, and then made his own fortune as well.

So he could get away with this kind of bad behavior. The only person who would have scolded him for it, who would have reminded him having money didn't make you better than other people, was dead. All that was left of her, their son, was now perhaps on the verge of death as well.

It was the thought of Tassin that spurred Embriem on. The butcher's boy was staring at the coin, hesitating. "Within an hour," Embriem repeated. Then he turned and strode out, causing the small bell on the door to jingle as he stepped into the thin fog that hung beyond the threshold. As he stepped outside, he heard a larger bell. Its silvery notes pealed out over the town, three brisk rings, letting everyone know a merchant ship had come into harbor.

Embriem paused on the threshold, a desperate hope sparking in his chest. He turned to hurry towards the shortcut up the hillside that would take him to the harbor.

On the sea, the fog had been chilly. As Marim walked up the rise from the small harbor, that changed. As she crested the hill and began to descend, the temperature rose. She got the feeling she'd have had a grand overlook of the island had the fog not obscured her view.

Not that Marim was much in the mood for grand views. The very word *island* filled her with an unpleasant sensation of dread, and the uncomfortable reality only sank in a little more with each step she took.

She was on the island of Cynnes Tarth. Here she was, a girl who had never so much as seen the ocean until a few months before, and she was stranded on a small piece of land surrounded by water and shrouded in fog.

The merchant vessel would stay in the harbor for a few weeks. Knowing this eased Marim's discomfort slightly. Though she doubted the captain would change his mind about her now, there was always a chance. She would go back tomorrow and speak with him again. Every day, she would go back. If she was persistent enough, perhaps he would relent.

It was the only plan she had.

For now, Marim needed somewhere to stay. The town of Lan Dinas, she'd been told, could be reached by following the road that left the docks. So she walked alone in the strange silence brought down by the fog. The harbor was not far behind. She'd left it mere moments before, but she could no longer see or hear any evidence of the activity that surrounded the ship. She walked in a bubble of quiet, the salt tang fading from the air. Around her, the landscape was a riot of green dimmed by the gray air.

When she'd first stepped off the ship, Marim had felt unsteady. Now she was adjusting to the sensation of being back on solid ground. But that was little comfort. With each step she took, her sense of dread grew.

The problem was, this was not the outcome Marim had foreseen. She'd intended to stay with the ship for months, or maybe even years. Masidon was rebuilding. Trade with the Fog Isles was flourishing again. There were fifteen major islands, Marim knew, arranged in an arc. The merchant vessel she'd chosen had plans to stop at many of them. She'd wanted to be with the ship, to see the exotic edges of known civilization before returning to the shores of her own country.

Cynnes Tarth, where she was now marooned, was the largest island in the string, and the nearest to Masidon. That was all she knew about the place.

She walked on. The track bent this way and that, smaller tracks splitting off at intervals. There were no signposts to point the way. The landscape hardly changed. Marim experienced a feeling of vertigo accompanied by a flash of irritation. She repressed the urge to swipe her hand in front of her face in an attempt to clear the air. How did people find their way when they couldn't see more than ten feet in any direction?

The irritation was only partly her own. Some of it came from Kix, who was curious about this new place. Her tessila hadn't liked the ship at all. He'd found it boring, her desire for him to stay near her restrictive, the lack of vegetation unsettling.

Now, Kix wanted to come through the stitchring and see the island. Marim was keeping him persuaded to stay where he was with some difficulty. His desire to defy her wishes was a needling burr in her thoughts. She was fairly certain the majority of the people here would be unfamiliar with tessili. After what had happened with the sailors, she was determined not to show Kix to anyone. She needed introductions to go well if she was going to be stranded here.

Still, as Marim walked, she couldn't help but think it would have been a comfort to see her tessila's small bright yellow body flitting and darting about, adding a tiny spark of brilliance to the muted palette of the landscape. She would have liked to feel his uncomplicated fascination with his new surroundings. Kix had nearly died once, years ago. He'd been different since then—a little simple—his emotions superficial and changeable, his thoughts shallow, his magic crippled. In spite of all their years at the academy, he never seemed to learn anything. Marim had never been able to get him to change size like all the other bound tessila could do.

Kix was damaged goods. Just like Marim herself.

At this thought, Marim's hand strayed to the top of her cloak. The scars around her neck were faint. She knew that. She also knew the light in this place would work to her advantage. Anyone she met was unlikely to notice her disfigurement. Still, she pulled her bunched hood a little closer around her throat.

She kept walking. The road flattened out. And then, all of a sudden, there was a building ahead of her. It loomed out of the fog so quickly, Marim came to an abrupt halt. She blinked and saw more buildings beyond the first, only the faintest of outlines.

She had reached Lan Dinas.

There was only one town on the island. The captain, in his apologetic attempts to convince her his decision to leave her here was for her own good, had stressed it was a nice town, prosperous, with a large cloister that educated the children and a thriving upper-class made up of merchants and tradesmen.

Now, the fog lent the street a fairytale quality. Recovering from her surprise, Marim continued forward, following the road as it widened into a cobbled street. The structures were tidy, painted bright white with colorful accents, as if trying to overcome the gray air. She couldn't see very far in any direction, which made the street seem deserted. She felt as if she'd stumbled upon a ghost town.

Marim scanned the houses and shops as she passed. "White house, yellow trim, porch with a double staircase." She muttered these words under her breath, her heart beginning to pound with uncertainty. The captain had suggested, delicately, the pub near the harbor was not a place a respectable female would prefer to stay. He'd told her of a private home in town that took only female lodgers, but he also conceded it had been years since he last sent someone there.

What if the house the captain had described was no longer accepting travelers? She supposed there was always the cloister, but Marim would only go there if she grew desperate.

She had made it past half a dozen structures when she heard footfalls behind her. Resisting the urge to whirl around, Marim stopped and looked over her shoulder. She saw a man approaching. He walked with purpose, his strides long and energetic. He was breathing heavily, as if he'd been running. She stopped walking, unnerved by the intense way he was looking at her. She was certain she'd never seen him before, and yet he approached without hesitation.

Startled, even a little scared, Marim took a step back. The man, seeing her expression, stopped a few paces away. He spoke in a breathless voice, not bothering with any kind of preamble. "Are you the healer?" he said. "From the ship?"

Tassin hadn't meant to disobey his father. Or his mother, for that matter. What his mother might have wanted him to do was harder to be certain of, since she was dead now, and had been dead for Tassin's entire life, excepting the few minutes between when he was born and she died.

The problem was, Tassin was hungry. He was so hungry he couldn't think of anything else. The hunger was like a lathe turning inside his belly. Tassin knew about lathes because his grandfather had one. It had taken Tem Cutter months to build the machine. While he'd been doing that, he'd had the blacksmith work on crafting him all sorts of special knives. Tassin's grandfather used to be a woodcutter—the most successful one on the island—but he'd retired at last. Now he worked wood younger men brought in from the forest, safe in the workshop attached to the back of his small home.

Tassin had seen the way the sharpened blades in his grandfather's hands sheared through the spinning wood as if it were soft as butter, scoring off long shavings that flew into the air to land in papery coils. He found it fascinating to watch the raw chunks of wood transform into delicate shapes as if by magic.

Tassin felt as if the same thing was happening to him. Something invisible was working away in his own stomach, whirling and biting and clawing and making him smaller.

They'd run out of food at home. They'd run out of food because Tassin couldn't stop eating. He ate and ate as if he'd grown a hollow leg, like his grandmother said. At first, it had been kind of funny. His father had said he was going through a growth spurt. He said he could remember being a boy himself and the long days watching the goras. Sometimes he'd eat his lunch too early and by evening think he couldn't get any hungrier.

But Tassin wasn't growing. He was doing the opposite. Day by day, the hunger raged through him and his body withered. A few days after it started, his other grandmother, the scribe, came to visit. She'd taken one look at him and sent word to the cloister.

Tassin did not like the cloister. His father took him there sometimes to light a candle for his mother's spirit. The boy found it hard to settle his thoughts like he was supposed to. The sisters of Delari unnerved him with the way they stared and smiled, showing their teeth.

The physician from the cloister was a lean woman with sharp eyes and strong, blunt hands like a man's. She examined Tassin and said he had the wasting disease, or maybe worms. He must eat as much as he could, and drink a tonic twice a day.

That had been three days ago. At least, Tassin thought it had been three days. It was getting hard for him to separate days from nights. He couldn't sleep properly. He couldn't wake properly either. All he seemed able to do was look at things and think about whether or not he could eat them.

This morning, he'd had a massive breakfast. His father had watched, his face growing pale, as Tassin devoured anything put within reach. "It shouldn't be possible," he said. "Where is it all going?"

Tassin didn't know where it was going, only that he was hungry unless he was eating, and he was hot as well. His skin seemed to burn. At night he lay in his sheets with the windows open, sweating and trying not to whimper with the pain of his empty belly. During the day, he ate everything his father could bring him. It was never enough.

This morning, Tassin had eaten his way through the eggs his one grandmother brought and the bread his other grandmother brought and the slab of smoked ham his father had purchased the day before. When the food was gone, his father had said, "Come here."

They'd been in the kitchen, which was a large clean space kept spotless by Secha, the cook. Until recently, Tassin's nurse would have been the one mostly taking care of him, but she'd left a few months before to help with her new grandchild. He was five now. His father said he wouldn't get another nurse, but a proper governess to see about his education.

For now, though, the large house Tassin and his father lived in had three servants. There was Secha, who lived up the street but came every day to make lunch and dinner, and there was Baret, who lived in the room off the back hall and kept the gardens and all the rooms that weren't the kitchen in working order. Finally, there was Krisin, a young lady who came every day to clean anything that needed cleaning and handle laundry and mending and making the beds and things like that.

There were Tassin's grandmothers as well. They were forever stopping by to bring fresh bread or fruit, to sit or play with Tassin and tell him stories. Sometimes, they asked him questions. Was he lonely? Did he have friends? Didn't he want to go outside more often?

But Tassin didn't mind his quiet life. He wasn't prone to mischief, as his grandmother said his father had been as a boy.

Which made what he was doing this morning exceptionally strange.

Tassin's father had gone out not long after breakfast. He'd left after he'd told the boy to come to him. He'd wrapped his fingers around his son's wrist and felt how little flesh there was on top of the bone. He'd lifted the boy's shirt and stared at his jutting hips, his protruding ribs. Then he'd surged out of his chair in a rush, saying, "I'm going to the butcher's. Stay here."

His father had gone, leaving Tassin to stare at the closed door. Neither Secha nor Krisin had come yet. Baret was out in the back garden. It wasn't the first time Tassin had been left mostly to his own devices, but it was the first time he disobeyed his father's direct orders.

When Embriem left, Tassin waited a few minutes, the hunger curling and clawing through his body. Then he slid out of his seat, went into the front hall and stood staring for a time at the large front door. The house was silent and empty and large. There was no one to stop him. So Tassin did what he'd been wanting to do for days. He opened the door and left the house, determined to go to the warmlake.

Tassin didn't know why he wanted to go to the warmlake, only that it was in his thoughts almost as strongly as the desire to eat. He wanted to walk down the long grassy slope to the spit of sand where his father told him his mother had used to take her washing when she was just a girl. He wanted to wade into the warm water and hear the small cries and plops of the brinlins as they climbed about in the reeds and dropped into the water. He wanted to stand in the water and … what? He didn't know what he wanted to do, only that it was important.

His mistake was not putting on his shoes. He didn't think of it until he left the house, and then he didn't want to go back for fear Baret would hear him. So Tassin kept going, feeling the cool, rough cobbles of the long drive beneath the soles of his feet, walking along at an energetic rate and trying to look as if he was doing something his father had told him to do rather than exactly the thing his father had told him not to.

The fog was thin and warm. He made it to the end of the lane his house was at the top of and onto the road that circumnavigated town. He sped up, growing excited as he made progress towards his goal. At last, he made it onto the narrow track that led down to the warmlake.

It was there he passed Layne Gordom. He didn't stop when he saw her, only kept on walking. He did nod, though, to be polite.

Layne did not keep walking. As he went past, she stopped and turned around to look at him, eyes narrowed. "Tassin," she said before he could get far enough away to pretend he couldn't hear her. "Where are you going?"

Tassin was an honest boy. This fact was his downfall. He should have thought about this possibility. He should have had an answer prepared. But he hadn't, and now his mind was stuck. He stared, mute, unable to think of a lie. All he could think about was how he didn't like Layne Gordom. His father said she was unhappy, but Tassin thought she was just mean.

When he couldn't answer, the woman frowned, stomped up to him, and took him by the wrist. She began to walk back the way he'd come, all but dragging him along beside her. She told him his father would be angry and his mother, had she been alive, would have been disappointed. She said this over and over as she hauled Tassin back up the lane.

Tassin went with her, but he stopped listening to her words. All he could think about was how they were going the wrong way, and he was so very hungry.

⊹

The Rooster's Comb did not typically open until noon. Cockram was unloading a crate of whiskey bottles when he heard the bell announcing the arrival of a merchant ship in the harbor. It was mid-morning, but he turned with a sigh and a grunt, glancing around the common room. "Tilde," he barked, "put down the fresh rushes. Now." Then he strode across the room and unlocked the door, swung it wide, and leaned out to flip the little sign outside from "closed" to "open."

He heard a rustle as he turned back around. Tilde was there, walking across the room with a rag in her hand. His daughter favored her mother, with her long neck and her willowy way of walking. She'd been a sweet child, but lately she'd gained a new aspect. There was a certain sullen, rebelliousness to the way she looked and spoke to him. It was subtle, nothing he could call her out on, but it grated on his nerves and made his temper shorter than usual.

"The reeds, girl," he snapped as she wandered past the tables. She never hurried, no matter how he prodded. Sometimes he could swear she was carrying out her tasks as slowly as possible with a focused deliberateness that set his teeth on edge.

Tilde did not respond. She tossed her rag onto the bar and headed for the back door. In the yard behind the pub she would pull a bundle from the stack of fresh reeds, maneuver their bulk through the door, and scatter them across the floor.

Cockram began pulling chairs down from the tops of the tables and setting them upright. Taking the chairs down first would make Tilde's task more difficult, but that was her own fault for dawdling. Cockram was a firm believer in consequences. Everything a person did in life had consequences – a ripple of effects spreading out from each action. That day in the wood yard, for instance, so long ago, he'd first seen the woman he would later marry. He'd approached, smiling. She'd smiled back. That moment had brought him here, step by slow step.

Cockram heaved the last chair off the table as his daughter pushed through the back door carrying the reeds. Her eyes flicked over the chairs. He could have sworn her expression curdled a little. But she said nothing, did nothing but carry her reeds to the farthest corner of the room and begin to scatter them. They were good for this purpose. Soft and papery after drying, they were able to soak up spilled beverages and keep the floor from going slick as the night wore on.

Cockram returned to the bar, tossed Tilde's abandoned rag into the hamper, and fumed as he watched his daughter's lethargic efforts. Halfway through, he told her to go make sure all the water barrels were full and took over the job himself.

The first sailors began to arrive moments after he finished with the reeds. They pushed through the door in small groups, eyes sweeping over the taps and bottles arranged behind the bar. Cockram assessed the men as they settled at tables, pleased to see they all shared a tidy appearance. The port masters had standards, of course, and didn't allow ships with unruly crews to remain docked. But there were a lot of new vessels on the waters these days, and many seamen behaved differently when out from under the captain's eye.

Cockram didn't like sailors. He thought there must be something inherently wrong with any man who chose such an unmoored life. But you didn't have to like something to make a living off of it.

On a normal night, the Rooster's Comb was a quiet pub. The men who worked in the warehouses and on the docks would often stop for a drink or a meal on their way home. On fine days when the fog wasn't too thick, townsfolk would walk up from high street to have a beer and sit on the patio, where they could watch the waves heave in and out of the harbor. And of course, there were the small crews from the light luggers that scampered from island to island. They often took a room for a few nights, and Cockram knew dozens of them by name.

But on nights when a merchant vessel was in port, the place filled up. What would seem the entire crew would come in at once, cramming into the Rooster's small common room, filling tables, ordering drink after drink. Sometimes Cockram would send to town for the city guard. He'd give two or three of them free drinks their next day off in exchange for them hanging around the common room, visible in their uniforms. Their steadying presence helped keep the crowd less rowdy.

It usually worked, but not always. Sometimes fights would break out. A man had been knifed once, fatally. He'd bled out right there on the floor. It had taken Cockram months of sanding to get the stain out.

The men here today, however, were subdued. Most of them ordered food only, then retired to the tables with their stew and bread. They spoke in low tones. A few of them asked for beer as well, but sipped the foamy brew at a slow pace. As the common room filled, it remained strangely quiet. There was none of the raucous joking and high spirits that making landfall typically gave rise to in men like these.

Cockram circulated among them, collecting empty dishes and keeping his ears open. He caught snatches of conversation that piqued his interest.

"… be glad when we're back at sea."

"It's not a natural thing …"

"… can't believe the captain ever let her on in the first place."

Cockram returned to the bar, setting the dishes in the tub for Tilde to haul to kitchen. He began to wipe down the counter, his attention on the shifting conversations all around him. Something had happened on their voyage, something that hung over these men as surely as the fog hung over Cynnes Tarth.

Had Cockram's wife still been with him, she'd have picked up on this as well. She'd have inserted herself among the sailors already, making them feel easy and welcome. She'd have collected all the ship's gossip over the course of the evening. Then, when they went to bed with the pub settled and quiet for the night, she'd have passed it on to him.

Cockram couldn't rely on Tilde for such things. She was as sullen with the guests as she was with her father. And while Cockram could talk to men, it wasn't the same. Gossip needed a woman's touch.

He was staring at a table of subdued sailors when the captain arrived. He walked through the door quietly, flanked by his mate. His presence was instantly noted by his crew. There was a ripple of subtle movement as men sat up a little taller in their seats, straightened collars that might have gone rumpled. The sailors dropped their voices further, or fell silent.

Captain Tommin was a man of middle height and middle years. He had sad eyes and the rolling gait of one who has spent his life on the deck of a ship. His shoulders, while broad, were a little stooped. He walked to the bar and pulled out a stool. Cockram knew him. He'd been in an out of this port for the last thirty years. His ship, up until recently, had been one of less than half a dozen left that could make the crossing to Masidon.

The captain spoke before Cockram could greet him. His words were strange, as was his tone. "There's a house in town, isn't there? White, with yellow trim? That takes women to lodge?"

Cockram considered the question. He looked at the tidy sailors with some uncertainty. "Captain Tommin." He smoothed his neck scarf, adjusting the golden rooster pin he wore there. "I'm honored by your presence in my humble establishment. We have rooms for any passengers you might have aboard."

His was the only pub on the waterfront. While there was no hard and fast rule against sailors going into town, they were discouraged from doing so. The people of Lan Dinas were not keen on outsiders.

"She's not my passenger." Tommin spoke with an odd strain in his voice. "She was to be healer on my vessel." He trailed off, not explaining further.

Cockram's curiosity was piqued now. He pulled a draft of beer and set it before the captain. "Any physician would be more than welcome at the cloister," he said. "We have a fine …."

The captain cut him off. He didn't do it in an aggressive way. Rather, his words were so quiet Cockram could barely make them out. "She's not a physician." There was a pause as Cockram tried to decide what to make of this. The captain repeated, "She's a healer." Then, in the growing silence he added, "I thought she might make me a globe runner, eventually, though she's young yet, and inexperienced."

It took a few moments for Cockram to parse what this meant. When he understood, a bolt of fear and shock shot through him. He stood up straighter, feeling his temper spark.

He'd heard rumors, of course. It had been a dozen years, maybe more, since brand new ships from Masidon began to arrive in Cynnes Tarth, bringing trade and stories. The sailors spoke of the war that had ravaged their distant homeland. The tales were varied, many of them incoherent, but everyone agreed on one thing – the Tessilari had risen again. It was their magic, after all, that allowed vessels to navigate the Two Trials.

Still, knowing a ship operated with the help of a guideglobe was one thing. Learning a Tessilar had made landfall, was right here on his island, was quite another.

Cockram leaned forward, trying to catch the captain's eye. But the man wouldn't look at him. He was staring at the foam on the beer as it sighed and sank. Cockram spoke anyway, not even trying to keep the horror out of his voice. "You brought one of them here? I tell you now, she'll find no welcome in Lan Dinas. Keep her on your ship, and take her with you when you go."

The captain did look up then. Something had gone hard in his eyes. "She's a person, same as any other. She'll do you no harm." He reached into his jacket and drew out a folded piece of paper to slide across the counter with a coin set on top. "Give this to Vailria, will you?"

Then he left, pushing back from the bar and leaving the beer untouched.

In response to some invisible signal, his crew followed. They stood, one after the other, some only halfway through their food or drink. They filed out, silent to a man.

An hour later, Cockram heard the single toll of the harbor bell that meant the great ship had left.

CHAPTER 2

The town of Lan Dinas was built on the fertile stretch of land between the seaside and the warmlake. It was not a flat expanse of space, but sloped. The streets all ran on angles, cobbled and narrow and steep.

From her window in the second story of the house that belonged to Embriem, Marim imagined she'd be able to see the warmlake if it not for the fog. The house was situated at the top of High Street, with a large back garden that opened up to the steep hillside that separated the city from the harbor. Marim gathered it was a fine house by the standards of Lan Dinas, though it was simple and modest compared to the elaborate architecture of even the more subdued estate houses in the Administrative City in Deramor.

She'd been in this house for three days. Any hope she'd had of changing Captain Tommin's mind was long dead. The treacherous man had lied to her about his plan to stay in port for several weeks.

His ship was gone. Embriem had told her. It had sailed away mere hours after she left its deck.

Standing in front of the open window, Marim watched Kix flit about in the summer warm, fog-choked air. It was a risk, letting him out, but her tessila was growing stir crazy with too much confinement. First, the weeks on the ship after the incident, during which Captain Tommin had diplomatically suggested she stay in her cabin as much as possible so as to give the crew little reason to dwell on how she'd almost gotten them all killed. Now, she was spending every waking moment with the boy whose life she was supposed to save.

It was an early morning in late summer, the sun beginning to light up the heavy air with its slanted rays. The fog had a smell: a dusky, coppery scent that somehow reminded Marim of swimming in the river behind Tessili Academy on a sunny day. It was an odd association, since the sun had not so much as touched her skin since the ship had plunged into the bank of fog that clung to Cynnes Tarth.

Three days. Could it really only be three days since she followed Embriem to his house, prepared to meet a boy with a simple case of wasting or worms? She'd been pleased then, following Embriem up the steep street to his house, thinking how she'd woo the people here by treating their small ailments, one by one. She would be more careful than she'd been with the sailors. She would keep Kix hidden, pretend to collect herbs and mix tinctures, then use her healing magic to banish their ills and heal their wounds. Not until she'd gained their trust would she tell them she was Tessilari.

It had seemed a good plan, right up until the moment she saw the boy.

On the walk up to the house, Embriem had introduced himself and explained his son's trouble. He'd asked her if she would be willing to stay in his home and monitor the boy until he was well again. Although the man's manner was distracted and his clothing a little untidy, his shirt was of a fine, heavy material, his boots of soft, supple leather and his tone and manner that of a gentleman. She'd accepted his offer without hesitation. She had nowhere else to go, after all.

They'd reached the house, and Embriem had given her over to a servant who led her to this room. She'd unpacked a few things and freshened up. An hour later the same man had come again and led her to a large, dim sitting room where young Tassin awaited her examination.

She'd gone downstairs with a sense of ready confidence. This had shattered and fallen to pieces the moment Embriem had turned to her from beside a low couch saying, "Marim, this is my son, Tassin, who I've brought you here to help."

The sight of the boy had taken her breath away. He was much, much too thin. His head seemed huge, his eyes overlarge, his wrists and elbows and knees thick knobs in withered limbs. His eyes were a brilliant, startling blue, his hair light and fine, as if spun of sunlight.

"Tassin," Embriem said, "this is Marim. She's a healer, a very good one. She's come a long way to help you get better."

The words were not true. Marim felt her heart clench at the hope in the man's voice. She was not a good healer. She wasn't a bad healer either. She was merely a weak healer. She was weak at healing because her magic was weak in all applications. She was, as far as she knew, the weakest Tessilar in existence.

It was part of why she'd left Masidon. She was tired of being the one everyone pitied, tired of failing at the simple spells everyone else could toss off without effort. She'd thought if she went where there were no other Tessilari at all, she would be the strongest by default and thus her skills, modest as they were, would no longer seem so pathetic.

Only that wasn't how things were working out. First, the disaster on the ship. Now this.

As she'd stared across that room, Marim felt horror take root in her chest. This was not a boy with worms. This was not a boy with a wasting disease. This was a boy with the hunger, and the hunger meant only one thing.

Feeling like the worst sort of imposter in the history of the world, Marim examined the boy: touching his thin wrists, feeling the weight of his starved gaze on her skin. She wore a blouse with a high collar. Still, she had to resist the urge to pluck at it, to make sure it covered her neck. She'd gotten through that initial introduction somehow, mumbled something about checking her sources, and hurried from the room.

Now, watching Kix turn in flight, Marim felt the heavy stone of dread in her stomach. Three days watching the boy wither before her eyes. Three days casting desperately about for some answer, some solution, other than the one that was both obvious and impossible. She'd read through her entire spellbook, knowing it would do no good. And it hadn't. It only reminded her how much basic magic continued to be beyond her ability.

She moved to the desk. Its surface was bare except for a slim cherry wood case. She reached for this and opened it, feeling the spark of magic in the clasp as it recognized her touch. With her heart in her throat, she lifted out the three smooth leather tablets and lined them up to read.

The first bore the crest of Tessili Academy in the lower corner, and it was blank. She'd wiped it clean after she'd reported her safe arrival in Cynnes Tarth and the academy had confirmed receipt of her message.

The second was covered in writing: all the frenzied questions she'd flung at Professor Liam since she'd discovered Tassin had the hunger. His answers were sympathetic and practical, but not terrible helpful. "You can boost him with active vitality spells, but do not overextend yourself. He must find a tessila or he will die." Her reply, "There are no tessili on this island." His response, "Then he is lost. I'm sorry, Marim."

The third tablet was blank except for the question she'd written at the top three days ago. "Made it to Cynnes Tarth. Have met a boy dying of the hunger. How is this possible?"

Professor Liam was learned and wise. He'd studied tessili and magics his entire life. She should accept his word, admit to Embriem she could not help.

Yet Marim found she could not do so. Not yet. She'd asked Embriem's gardener if any brillbane grew on the island. The man had seemed puzzled by her query, but said he would look out for it and ask around.

Besides, there was still the third tablet. It remained empty. As she stared uselessly at the blank space below her question, she felt the stone of dread turn into a boulder. Absently tracing the texture of the scars on her throat with an idle finger, she murmured into the quiet of the room. "By Delari's breath, Coll. Check your tablet already."

✛

She waited for a quarter of an hour, hoping. But the third tablet remained lifeless, no reply appearing beneath her query. At last, she could delay no longer. She returned to the window and looked out, straining for a glimpse of Kix's bright yellow hide in the glowing air. She could feel him out there, flying in loops. He'd gone farther away than he usually did. She called him back with a mild sensation of alarm. He could be impulsive – a trait they shared.

He came indirectly, taking long, coiling detours. He did not want to spend another day hiding in her sleeve. He wanted to fly, to find other tessili and play chase. He didn't like the fog or the quiet, empty landscape. He wanted sunlight and the river and dozens of brillbane bushes to perch on instead of just the one the stitchring allowed him to reach.

She spoke to him as he made his grudging return. "And I want my scars and your scars to disappear. I don't want to be weaker than even a first year initiate. I want you to be able to shift." She could feel the cool tickle of the fog on her face as she leaned out the window.

At last, Kix landed on her outstretched hand, gripping her thumb with his tiny pinpricks of talons. He cocked his head to regard her with a brilliant black eye. In this light, the marred scales around his shoulders and across his back stood out. She felt the familiar clench in her heart at the visible evidence of his maiming.

They were both scarred, but the worst damage was internal.

She spoke to him, her words coming out harsh with her disappointment at not hearing back from Coll. "What we want and what we get are two different things."

Kix settled his wings with a grumpy air and crawled up her sleeve to sulk. Marim checked herself in the mirror, adjusted her collar one last time, and went downstairs.

She found Tassin in the sitting room, curled on the low couch where he'd spent most of his time since she'd arrived. His appetite was beginning to wane – a sign the end was growing near.

Marim regarded the boy's tousled head from across the room, feeling a deep sadness turn over within her. She remembered her own time with the hunger, the terror in her parents' eyes, the fleeing to her grandparents' cheesery and the desperate days that followed as first her mother, then her father, developed the same affliction.

She'd been five years old, and hadn't understood what was happening. She only knew she was in pain and her parents stank of fear and she was not allowed to go outside or see her friends or speak to anyone.

Then, one evening she went to bed to thrash and shift endlessly on the narrow cot her grandparents had set up for her in a small storage room, hunger clawing her from the inside. In the morning, she awoke not to the shelves of maturing cheeses and the scent of clover and whey, but a sun-filled bedroom with a vaulted ceiling, huge bright windows, and potted brillbane growing on every side. She'd been too weak by then to wonder much at the change. She hadn't known a word for the plants, then, or the tiny, flying creatures that filled the air, their brilliant hides catching the light, but she'd been unable to take her eyes off them.

There had been a man sitting in a straight wooden chair pulled up to her bedside. Wearing a soft brown robe, he'd watched her with kind eyes. He'd set a cool hand on her forehead and spoken in a low, soothing voice. "They're called tessili. Do you like one of them in particular?"

She'd noticed Kix, then. The yellow tessila had seemed aware of her as well. Too enchanted to remember how weak she was, forgetting her hunger for the first time in days, Marim sat up, half convinced it was a dream. Kix wheeled on the air and came to her. As he alighted for the first time on her outstretched hand, something broken in Marim's soul healed itself clean over.

Kix had looked at her. He was perfect, then, his hide not yet marred by the scars of the harness. She was not yet scarred either, though she would have been if she'd know how she'd come to be in that place. She smiled at the tiny creature, feeling suddenly full of warmth and potential. His name filled her mind like one, perfect, plucked note on a harp. *Kix. His name is Kix.*

The man, his face benevolent, reached for a tray waiting on a side table. "How about something to eat?"

She ate with gusto, but not desperation. Her hunger had been cured, somehow, by Kix.

She didn't know then, wouldn't know for years, what had happened. In the coming days, she would learn the rhythm of the academy, and the place would swallow her whole. She had only a scattering of pale, muddled memories of her time there. She'd certainly had no way of knowing one of the other students, someone she shared mealtimes with and passed in the quad, had crept into her grandparents' house that night, murdered her parents, and stolen Marim away.

Now, decades later, Marim looked at Tassin and felt the old, familiar conviction creep into her mind, dark and slippery and full of heavy horror. It was a thought that had nested next to her heart for years.

She should have died of the hunger, like Tassin would. It would have saved the world an awful lot of grief.

But Marim had not died. Not then, when she'd come so close. Not later, when she and Kix had hovered between life and death for days, not a few weeks ago when her idiocy had trapped Captain Tommin's ship in the first of the two trials and they'd drifted, doomed.

Now, standing in this dim room, she seemed to hear Professor Liam's voice in her head, answering her now the way he'd done when she'd confessed this dark conviction to him before she left the academy. He'd taken her outpouring in stride, saying, "If it hadn't been you, Nylan would have taken a different initiate. The same thing would have happened."

But was it true? Nylan had chosen her for some reason. Perhaps another girl would have fought harder, managed to free herself, refused to do what Nylan said, died instead of unleashing a horror on the world. "What happened was not your fault," Liam said. "Surely you can see that."

On the couch, Tassin shifted, turning to look at her with his feverish eyes. Marim shook herself, pushing her heavy thoughts to the corners of her mind. This boy was not dead yet. For now, she would do what she could.

She went to him and sat, taking his hand and mustering the best active vitality spell she could manage. She focused on the weave of the magic, pulling and dragging at her scrambled bond with Kix. She released the spell and it took, giving Tassin a small boost of life.

The effort left her breathless. Marim leaned back in her chair and closed her eyes. The room was silent and cool, filled with the smell of polished wood and the distant spice of the fog.

They sat a moment, breathing, until Tassin spoke up, surprising her. "Is that a brinlin?"

Marim's eyes flew open. She stared down at her sleeve in horror. Kix had poked his head past her cuff to fix his keen eyes on Tassin. The tessila withdrew as soon as the boy spoke, scrambling up the inside of her sleeve, his needle-sharp talons pricking her tender skin.

Tassin looked a little better. His eyes were clear and alert, and he was staring at the spot Kix had been as if he'd seen a unicorn. He waited a moment, then looked up at her with expectation.

Marim, mouth dry, couldn't find any words. His blue eyes held hers for a few heartbeats.

There was a quiet shuffle at the door. Baret the gardener peeked into the room. "Sorry to interrupt, young miss. But I've been looking and asking all over for the plant you mentioned. Is this it?"

Vailria could never smell the sea without experiencing the strange blend of joy, desire, nostalgia, and loss she associated with

Tommin. It was a heady cocktail, always accompanied with an aftertaste of bitterness. This morning the rush passed in an instant, while the sharp flavor of disappointment lingered.

It was a long walk from Vailria's little house on the shore of the warmlake up to the harbor. As she crested the rise that separated town from sea, the air and the fog took on the scent of brine. She continued down, walking and straining to see through the fog. When one of the great merchant vessels occupied the port, its many masts would tower high into the misty air, dwarfing the local luggers and barges tied up nearby.

Today, there was no such vessel waiting in the docks. Vailria already knew this. Six months, he'd been away. And now, she'd missed him. She didn't understand. Usually, when Tommin put in at Cynnes Tarth, he lingered for weeks. His ship was massive, which meant heaps of cargo to load and unload. She'd walked the holds with him herself, running fingers over bolts of exotic fabric, breathing in the dusty tang of the spice hold. All day, he would trade and barter, buy and sell. All night, he would be hers.

At the start of each such interlude, being with Tommin was all joy. But the weeks would pass and the sailors would grow restless and each day her heart would grow a little heavier with the dread of what must come. Finally, he would say the terrible words. "I must leave with the morning tide."

Then they would have the conversation – the one they'd had over and over these 30 years. He would ask her to marry him. She would refuse to wed a man she did not see for months or years at a time. She would ask him to stay. He would say, "Another trip or two. Then I'll have enough put by. I'll repay my investors, sell this ship and everything left on it. We'll start our new life. Soon."

The first time he'd said it, they'd been 19. And she'd believed him. She still believed him, each time he made the promise. She believed him when he was there, a flesh and blood man lying in the tangle of sheets beside her. It was when he was gone, reduced to nothing but a shade in her mind, she found herself filled with doubt.

Sometimes she decided she could not wait any longer. Sometimes she decided to make him stay, to set her hand on his arm and give him a little nudge in the right direction. She fantasized about doing this when he was away. It would be so easy. And after it was done they'd both be happier, she was sure.

But she hadn't done it. She would never do it. It wasn't that she could not, or that she believed she would regret it, after the fact. It was the slippery reality that if she intervened, if she touched her lover's feelings for her in any way, she would never have the satisfaction of knowing he'd stayed because it was what he chose.

Still, 30 years was getting to be a long time to wait. And now, this anomaly. Tommin and come to Cynnes Tarth. His vessel had docked and his men had come ashore but he'd left before she had time to come to him.

She'd been in Gol Ledrith making her quarterly report to the Circle and fulfilling various other social and professional obligations. When she saw he was near, she'd been disappointed to know she would miss his first few days in port. But she'd thought they'd still have several weeks. Or maybe, at last, he would stay and they would have the rest of their lives.

Only his ship left again the very day it put in. Everyone in Lan Dinas was talking about it, rumors flying about a conflict with the port authority. Captain Tommin was well known and well liked in town. Her first day back, Vailria spent the whole day listening, trying to understand. But it was groundless gossip. No one knew anything for certain.

Now, here she was, standing on the stone quay and gazing at the heavy waters of the ocean as if they could tell her what it meant. Was it a message? Was Tommin telling her they were through?

Nostrils full of brine, Vailria paced back and forth along the docks several times before realizing she was only torturing herself, coming here. Pulling her cloak in around her body, she turned and started back up the road that led to town.

Outside the harbor, she passed the Rooster's Comb. It was a tidy pub with a painted sign out front, a large door, and heavy furniture arranged on the patio for a view of the muffled, heaving sea. A man was outside, sweeping. He looked up as Vailria approached and went still, his broom stopping mid sweep.

Vailria knew the man, and her blood curdled at the sight of him. Cockram. Brother of Adni. A man who feared his own potential and was made mean by that fear.

Her cloak had a passive echo spell woven into the fabric. It didn't make her invisible, particularly not when she had the hood down, but it did smudge her a bit. Most people would not approach her when she had it on, and also would not remember seeing her if she did not speak to them or do anything interesting.

She would have walked by Cockram and continued back to town without stopping, but he surprised her by calling her name just after she passed. She stopped, but did not turn to look at him. Instead, she closed her eyes and felt at the air between them, studying it for clues.

Cockram's voice was a sneer when he spoke again, throwing his words at her unguarded back like poison darts. "Looking for your handsome captain?"

Vailria's heart began to beat a little faster. She felt a spark in his words, and understood. This man knew something. Something he did not intend to tell her.

Angry now, she turned and opened her eyes. Vailria was skilled in the passive arts, but direct and effective manipulation required touch. She took a step towards the patio, hazarding a guess. "Why haven't you delivered the message he left for me?"

Cockram leaned on his broom and watched her with his mean eyes, unapologetic. He looked smooth and well groomed, his sleeves rolled up and his forearms round with muscle. "The lady misunderstands me. I deal in brews, not words." As the sunlight shifted on the swirling fog, a gold pin in his neck scarf seemed to sparkle.

ROBIN STEPHEN

The anger was alive now, burning in Vailria's belly. She wanted to charge forward, grab this man's arm, and make him tell her what he knew.

But she could not. Even if it was not a violation of the Circle's laws, it was too dangerous by far.

He was playing with her. Nothing she could do or say would change his mind. She would not give him the pleasure of making her ask twice. Knowing that Tommin had left word for her was enough. Vailria would simply wait. She was good at waiting. Jaw clenched, she turned to go.

She could feel the man's delight in the pain he was causing her, rank on the breeze as rotting fish. As she took her first step away, he spoke in a speculative tone, basking in his own cruelty. "Tell me, Vailria. Why, after all these years, has Tommin never offered to take you with him?"

Vailria did not answer, did not look back. She wove a passive blurring spell and released it as she walked away, angry with this man, angry with Tommin, angry with herself for coming here.

She didn't bother to wait and watch her spell find its target. She was confident in what it would do. Vailria had power over memories of herself. The one thing she could reliably manage without touch was to wipe herself away, smudge any recollection in a person's mind in which she featured.

She walked briskly into the fog, but Cockram's final question chased her all the way back to Lan Dinas, filling her with worry.

It wasn't true, Tommin had asked her to leave Cynnes Tarth. Once. Long ago. Before he'd known what she was. Since she had explained, he had never asked again, because it would be the same as asking her to die.

As Vailria skirted the town, keeping to quiet side-streets where no one would see her, she wondered if Cockram was merely being cruel, or if he knew her secret.

Cockram watched Vailria fade into the fog, feeling the cold prickle of unease across his skin. Something about that woman filled him with dread.

She was walking away when he felt a strange trembling on the air. The gold pin he always wore in his neck scarf gave an odd twitch, as if tapped by an invisible finger. At the same time, he felt a sensation of vertigo. The fog seemed to grow suddenly thick. He stared at the empty street, filled with the vague impression he'd just been buffeted by a stiff wind.

Absently, he touched his pin to make sure it was secure, then snatched his fingers away with a curse, staring down at them in surprise.

The pin was hot. So hot, he could see two tiny red welts rising on his thumb and forefinger where the metal had burned him. He could also smell the flat scent of singed cloth.

In a convulsive jerk, Cockram dropped the broom and snatched at his neck cloth, pulling it free so the pin went flying. Holding up the fabric, he could indeed see a small, smoldering hole punched through in several places where the pin had penetrated.

He tossed the cloth onto a table and stood in the quiet morning, breathing hard. Vertigo washed over him and his mind felt suddenly muddled – blank of all thoughts but a series of vague impressions.

He stood, utterly still, for a long moment. His breathing slowed. The fog was a whispering touch against his skin. He shook himself and looked around.

His outdoors tables stood quietly nearby, their benches snugged up beneath them. But why was he out here at this time of day? He looked around for clues, and saw the broom at his feet.

Stooping, he picked it up. He needed to sweep the patio. A light storm had blown in off the sea in the night, leaving debris all over the stones.

Comforted by this explanation, Cockram began to sweep again. He returned to work as if he'd never stopped. Then he pushed a pile of leaves into the street, he saw a glint on the stones a few feet away. Curious, he stepped forward to take a look.

It was his rooster pin, caught in a crack between pavers. As Cockram laid eyes on the thing, he felt the hair on the back of his neck rise for reasons he could not explain.

He began to sweat. His mind balking and bucking like a spooked horse, Cockram felt a sort of disbelieving vertigo. He gazed down at the pin. It was solid gold, shaped into the form of a tiny rooster perched on a stump. It was rendered in breathtaking detail, the workmanship the finest he himself had ever seen.

He could remember the day he'd found the pin, hidden in a wooden box tucked beneath the false bottom of a locked chest in his father's closet. He'd been seven years old then, made rebellious by the death of his father followed so quickly by that of his sister. He'd stolen the pin, guessing correctly his mother wouldn't miss it. He'd kept it under his pillow for a time, a thrilling secret. Then he'd gotten tired of fearing he would lose it, and put it back.

It wasn't until the death of his mother shortly before his own wedding day that he found himself looking at his father's old chest and remembering the pin. He opened the false bottom, heart thrilling with hope, and found that familiar, worn box with its strange emblem. He opened it, removed the pin, and stuck it into his neck scarf.

He'd worn it every day since.

Now, he turned to look at his neck scarf tossed on one of the table tops, shifting in the sluggish breeze. Had he grown too warm? Pulled off the scarf and forgotten the pin? It made sense, but it didn't feel right. He was careful with the pin, protective.

Bending, Cockram picked the pin up. It was warm, and his fingertips were tender. The pin felt somehow alive beneath his skin, sending little tingling pulses up his arms. As he puzzled at this, the memories came back in a rush.

Vailria.

As if he'd heard a shout, Cockram whirled towards the road that connected Lan Dinas to the harbor, but it was empty. No woman walked there, watching him with flat eyes. It seemed to Cockram Vailria was everywhere in Lan Dinas, always tucked out of sight, listening, watching. Stranger still, no one else seemed to take much note of her.

He'd spoken to the rector about her more than once, and Dinon kept a list for her as he did for anyone who showed one of the signs the Directive bade him watch for. The woman lived on a little house on stilts, built out over the very water of the warmlake. Thus, she earned one mark practically by default.

But that was the only mark they could pin on her. She was aloof and antisocial. She was unpleasant and unfriendly, motivated by her own inexplicable agenda. But each time Cockram brought up her candidacy, Rector Dinon said the same thing. "We direct the hand of Tristis to cleanse Vestima's lingering rot. That is the sole purpose of the Directive. Without three marks, we cannot act. Do not let your dislike for this woman cloud your judgement."

Down in the harbor, one of the small bells clanged as a local lugger glided in from sea. Picking up the neck cloth, Cockram stared at the smoldering holes punched through the fabric. This would count as evidence of one inexplicable deed. But he needed three of those, observed within one month's time, before Dinon would bring another mark against Vailria and test her with the ring or the rod.

Annoyed, he shoved the scarf into his pocket, stuck the pin through his vest's lapel, and headed for the cloister.

Rector Dinon was a tall man with the lean build of one who walked much and ate little. His eyes were gray, overhung by severe brows drawn together in sympathy.

Embriem had never disliked him until today. While he himself was not particularly fervent in his devotions, he had always looked on the work of the cloister with vague approval. The sisters did a lot of good among the poorer circles of Lan Dinas, caring for the sick, educating any child who appeared at the cloister school with a desire to learn.

He was aware that, in some cases, the sick could not be healed. With wasting diseases in particular, a person could linger long on Tristis' doorstep, one foot in this world, one in the next, for months sometimes. In these cases, with the family's consent and Delari's blessing, the sisters would administer the death serum to release the afflicted from suffering.

Embriem could remember the first time he heard the tolling of the death bell. He'd been a boy, following his goras to the warmlake, when that aching note throbbed through the fog.

The tone of the bell had arrested him, echoing in his bones and tugging at his heart. He'd stopped short in the street to watch the somber procession go by. Rector Dinon, younger then, walked in the lead, his rich red robes muted by the fog. Behind him came the sisters in their black. At the very back, the physician in white. All of them walked with heads bowed in prayer.

He'd watched them go by, then hurried to catch up to his goras. The bell had gone out of his mind. Only later did he remember, when his father said to his mother, "Did you hear about the cobbler's boy? They've sent him on to Delari at last."

His parents had been in their sitting room, Embriem passing in the hall. He'd stopped in the doorway, feeling something strum in his sternum. The cobbler's boy had nearly drowned in the warmlake. They'd pulled him out and pumped the water from his lungs and he'd begun to breathe on his own again. But it had been weeks and he hadn't woken. "Sent him?" Embriem said, interrupting, which was rude, but unable to stop himself.

His had parents turned to look at him. His mother had given his father a hard look, then gestured to her footstool. "Come in and sit down."

She'd explained to him, then, how sometimes the kindest thing, the loving thing, is to let a person go.

Now, staring at the empty chair in his office Dinon had occupied a moment before, Embriem sat still, his thoughts all but fuzzed out by anger. Dinon had come to his house, knocked on his door, and asked to speak with him. Embriem had let him in, answered his questions, then listened as he spoke, his disbelief growing with every word that passed the man's lips. Yes, it had been seven days. Yes, Tassin had grown very thin. Yes, the physician's tonics did not help. Yes, Embriem loved his son and wanted to do right by him.

Then the terrible words, the pernicious suggestion. "In the church's experience, with these aggressive forms of the wasting, the last few days are very painful. It might be kindest to release Tassin before he arrives at that point."

Embriem had stared at the man, speechless. When he found his voice, he'd asked the rector to leave.

Dinon had said nothing at first, only smiled a kind, sad smile. Rising to go, he paused on the threshold. "Word has reached me the healer from the ship may be Tessilari. Did you know?"

Embriem, too overcome to speak, made no reply. The rector, red robes rustling, drew the sign of Delari's love in the air, turned, and left.

Embriem did not show him out. He remained in his seat, stunned, angry, lost. His eyes felt hot, his head thick. It was outrageous for the rector to have come to him so quickly. Surely, there was still time.

Down the entry hall, he heard the front door open and close as the rector left. He seemed to hear his mother's voice. *Sometimes the loving thing is to let go.*

Embriem sprang out of his chair as if it had grown hot. He rushed out of his office, energized but aimless. That word,

Tessilari, stuck in his mind. He'd heard the term before, of course. He even had a book in his library about tessili. His father had brought it home years ago, a curiosity he'd found in the collection of a deceased man whose entire library he'd purchased as a unit. Certain he'd never be able to sell the odd tome, he'd given it to his son.

Here, on Cynnes Tarth, the Tessilari were a distant rumor. Some believed they were a myth. But the guideglobes that allowed vessels to cross the two trials and survive the difficult voyage to Masidon were real enough, as was the magic that made them function.

Hurrying down the hall, Embriem made for his library. It took him a few minutes to find the volume. Tucked up on a high shelf, its spine cracked with age, he felt a strange sense of relief as he eased it into his hands.

The cover was plain leather with the word "Tessili" pressed into the front. It was a journal more than a proper book – the tale of some long-dead person's journey to Masidon. The inside was much as he recalled, though the drawings were more primitive, smaller, and less detailed. There was a sketch of a brillbane bush and quite a few of tessili, either in flight or perched on twigs or branches.

For a moment, Embriem lost himself leafing through the ancient pages. How old was this book? Dozens of years? Hundreds? He'd found it fascinating as a child, poring over the illustrations and descriptions many a rainy evening when he could not go outside.

It was not a thick book. He was nearing the end when he turned a page and saw a heading that made his heart throb with painful fear. It read, "The Hunger."

Embriem felt ice in his veins. The words seemed to shift on the page, blurring as his focus wavered. He blinked, drew in a deep breath, and read.

> *In some cases, the bond between tessili and human happens spontaneously. In other cases, the human is first afflicted with the hunger – a condition where the bonding pathway opens, but has no target. When this happens, if no tessila is available or receptive, the human will develop a voracious appetite that cannot be satisfied. The body will metabolize itself, leading eventually to death. Most often, this occurs in children around the age of five. But when one person develops the hunger, it can trigger the same affliction in other receptive humans with whom they come into close contact. Since the ability to bond is hereditary but may not manifest in those who are not exposed to tessili, it's not uncommon for entire families to develop the hunger at once.*

Embriem sat a moment longer as the ice in his blood gave way to fire. Anger surged through him, hot and quick.

Leaving the book on a table, trembling with rage, he went in search of Marim.

Marim thanked the gardener and sent him on his way. She stood for a moment after he left, preoccupied by the sour sensation of dying hope. She glanced at Tassin, but the boy had slipped into a light doze.

The plant wasn't brillbane. She held the sample in her fingers, turning it in the low light. She could see why the man had brought it to her. The leaves were thick and rounded. They connected to the stem in the right pattern. But they were much too small, and with none of the characteristic waxy coating.

Marim knew it was hopeless. According to both Professor Liam and the general query she'd sent to the tableturie, brillbane did not grow outside the valley of Deramor. It could be cultivated in greenhouses, but it did not thrive in such conditions. The magic of the tessili raised on greenhouse brillbane was not as potent. It was why the Tessilari were so excited about the new wild tessili population beginning to thrive. Many old powers, thought lost forever, were being rediscovered.

If there was no brillbane on this island, it meant there were no tessili. But if there were no tessili, why did this boy have the hunger?

Liam's theory was that old, old Tessilari blood ran in the boy's lineage. His aptitude for magics had somehow been triggered by mere happenstance. It happened, of course. Marim herself had never seen a tessila until after she'd been taken to the academy, but her hunger had surfaced anyway.

Still, Tassin looked as native to the Fog Isles as a person could. His fine hair, blue eyes, pale skin dashed over with freckles, light lashes and brows, soft features. If he had Tessilari blood, it did not show.

Turning, Marim stared at the boy with an increasing sensation of hopelessness. Outside, the fog shrouded the view. Marim felt stifled, trapped, and useless. What was she doing in this place? Why was she pretending she could save this boy when she could not?

Kix was on the other side of his stitchring, dozing in the unfiltered rays of sunlight that fell onto his brillbane bush. She pictured the academy, how it must look right now, with its green quad and its plentiful brillbane and all the tessili wheeling on the air as they flew in looping patterns.

She thought of Coll – the way he'd looked when she'd last seen him, standing and watching her leave, his dark eyes unreadable. He'd grown so tall last season. Though his magical ability had surpassed hers long ago, she was still the one he came to when he was excited or upset or wanted to show off. It had been that way since the moment he arrived at the academy, a frightened, lonely boy with a past that made the other students whisper about him when he wasn't there, and shy away when he spoke to them.

Marim knew how that felt, and he knew she knew. It was what connected them.

Heart leaden, Marim wondered what she would do when Tassin died. No one else would want her services as a healer if she lost her first patient. Captain Tommin had said he would return in a year or so. By then, he'd be ready to cross back to Masidon. He would allow her back onto his ship, to take her home.

It was generous of him, considering. But still, what would she do for a year in this place? How would she keep Kix hidden and secret? Already, her tessila was growing impatient with the way she was constantly restricting his movements.

Marim was stirred out of her thoughts by the sound of rapid steps in the hall. She turned to see Embriem, and the expression on his face made her heart leap with fear.

The man was angry. Furious, even. He paused on the threshold, glanced at Tassin, and gestured for Marim to follow him.

He led her into the back garden. The fog with its smell of summer teased her hair and clouded her vision. Embriem led her a short distance up a stone path, then turned. His words were sharp and hard, but not loud. "When were you going to tell me the truth? Or are you simply using my son's affliction to keep a roof over your head?"

Marim was so surprised, so hurt, tears sprang to her eyes. The accusation, accurate at its core, stung like the crack of a whip.

She felt her grip on herself slipping, the anger uncoiling from where it always rode lashed around her heart. Kix, feeling the sudden surge of her emotions, woke up.

But no. Embriem was wrong. Marim may not have found a way to help Tassin, but she'd been trying. She stared at Embriem, disbelieving. What right did he have to accuse her this way? She had done nothing since she'd set foot on this island but try to unravel the mystery. It wasn't her fault there was no solution to be found.

Too angry to be diplomatic, she hissed a reply through clenched teeth. "Your son would be dead by now if not for me. I have been boosting his vitality multiple times a day, draining myself to keep him going while I try to figure out where to find a tessila for him."

Embriem, taken aback by her anger, stared for a moment in silence. Marim stood seething. Why was she always the one forced into the role of villain? When Kix stirred, stretching his wings in preparation for coming back through the ring, she didn't try to stop him. She reached into her cloak and shifted the stitchring so it hung free of the fabric.

Embriem's eyes followed her movement. When Kix burst through the stitchring and wheeled through the air to land on her shoulder with an angry hiss, Marim felt a small ripple of satisfaction at the expression of utter shock on the man's face. He took a step backwards.

Good, Marim though, woozy with the cost of the spell that had brought Kix back to her. *Let him fear me.*

But the active vitality spells she'd been using to boost Tassin must have been taking more of a toll than Marim had realized. Instead of recovering from the stitchring's draw, Marim grew dizzier, her vision beginning to dim. She wobbled on her feet. Embriem, probably acting on reflex, reached out a hand to steady her.

She gripped his forearm. It was hard and firm. The wooziness faded and she found her balance again. She was about to let go, about to step back and away, when she felt something that made her go still with horror.

There was a rip in Embriem, a tiny tear through which his life force was beginning to leak. It was invisible, a flaw in the fabric of his very being. Marim recognized the feeling of it, because it was a milder version of what was killing his son.

Overtaken by new horror, Marim raised her eyes to the man's face. "Oh, Embriem." She could barely speak for the tightness in her throat. "Not you too."

CHAPTER 3

Marim wasn't prone to feelings of regret. If she had been, she'd never have survived the War of Diodsfall, never have learned to bear the terrible guilt over her part in it. Still, as she sat in her room two days after she'd discovered Embriem had the hunger as well, she couldn't help but wish she could go back to the moment she walked onto Captain Tommin's ship, full of hope and optimism, and begin again.

In retrospect, Marim saw how easy it would be to get along with the sailors, to avoid spooking them, to be more careful when Captain Tommin asked her to have a look at the guideglobe. All her great mistakes were this way. Looking back, she could see how easily her younger, more naïve self could have avoided the pitfalls. And then, if she hadn't alienated the sailors, they never would have put her off here. She never would have met Embriem. He never would have asked her to save his son.

Tassin was all but lost. He mostly slept now, sometimes writhing and muttering. She could still do a little to help him, to take the edge off his suffering. But she'd stopped trying to prevent the inevitable. How long would he linger? One more day? Two?

That morning, after visiting Tassin and doing what she could, she'd returned to her room and packed. She was aware Embriem might ask her to leave at any time. When that happened, she supposed she'd be forced to throw herself on the hospitality of the cloister.

It was a distasteful thought, but Marim had little recourse. Perhaps the sisters of Delari would let her help in the infirmary. Perhaps she could make herself useful until either Captain Tommin returned or another vessel agreed to take her home.

And then? She'd have to go back to Deramor, tail between her legs, the weakest Tessilar having failed even in her simple objective of seeing the world. She couldn't go back to the academy. She would have to return to the cheesery. She would accept Kix for what he was. She, too, would stop trying to be what she was not. She would learn to occupy the quiet, simple life her grandparents led.

Her tablets were spread out across the desk, her spellbook open beside them. She'd given up writing on them last night when she'd detected a hint of exasperation in the responses of the patient Professor Liam to her ceaseless queries. After speaking with Embriem, she could be certain. There were no tessili on Cynnes Tarth. There was no brillbane here. Which meant there was nothing left to talk about.

Still, she stared at the tablets. The first two were wiped clean of her correspondence with Professor Liam and the staff at the tableturie. The third had not changed since she'd arrived. At its top, in Marim's own hand, the question still sat there: "Made it to Cynnes Tarth. Have met a boy dying of the hunger. How is this possible?"

Annoyance surged through her. What was the point of Coll making such a show of giving her a tablet if he wasn't even going to check it now and then? Perhaps it wasn't working. He was still only a boy, after all. It took artifact makers years of study before they could reliably produce objects of such complexity. Although Coll's tablet looked like the other two, he claimed to have made it himself.

The anger, made restless by her gloomy thoughts, tightened in Marim's chest. She reached for the tablet, intending to chuck it out the window or throw it in the grate to be burned with the next fire. But before her fingers touched the leather, words began to appear.

They drew themselves letter by letter. Marim pictured Coll as he must look now, sitting at his desk in Tessili Academy, stylus gripped in his left hand, brow furrowed in concentration as he scored the words into the leather. Wip would be watching him work, or gnawing on a brillbane husk, or darting about the room, her matte bronze hide giving off a muted gleam in the lamplight.

Marim felt a lurch of homesickness strong enough to take her breath away. She lowered herself into the desk chair and closed her eyes, willing herself to wait until Coll had finished writing.

Around her, the house was still. Tassin would be downstairs, drifting in pain-filled slumber. Embriem wasn't allowing himself to eat more than usual, so he'd already lost a shocking amount of weight. He also wasn't allowing her to use any of her magic to bolster him. Marim suspected he would not outlive his son by long.

It didn't seem right, didn't seem possible. There had to be an answer, some detail she'd overlooked, some fact she didn't know. The anger uncoiled and bloomed through her, filling her with heat and frustration and a sense of helpless longing. Why, why, was she always too weak, too slow, too useless to do the right thing?

Unable to keep her eyes shut any longer, Marim let herself look for Coll's response. She'd expected a long reply, perhaps some speculation, or requests for details.

Instead, he had stopped after writing only one sentence. It was not an answer to her query, but a single question scrawled in his familiar, sloppy hand.

Marim stared at it, surprise overtaking all her other emotions and forcing them to stillness. Coll had answered her very serious question with eight words that seemed not at all connected to Tassin's troubles. "Have you been down to the warmlake yet?"

But Marim knew Coll better than to take this response at face value.

She had not been down to the warmlake. She'd hardly left this house.

Galvanized, she pushed out of her chair, grabbed her cloak, and headed for the door.

As a boy, Embriem had often fancied himself somewhat underfed. He'd wake up and have his breakfast, which would have been eggs and porridge and often some meat as well. He would then take his pack and follow the goras down to the warmlake, where he would watch the animals as they grazed. His lunch would be a small wheel of cheese, some bread, and a flask of watered wine, often with a sausage or a pie or some other extra treat.

It had never seemed like enough. Many days, Embriem felt hungry for hours before and after lunch. It had made it rather difficult to concentrate on the book his mother had given him, the one he was supposed to learn to read from.

In reality, though, the hungry phase had been brief. Embriem had grown out of it after reaching his full height. He'd still get hungry, just not the way he had for a while.

But now, looking back, he realized he'd never known hunger before. Not then. Not ever.

Now, Embriem was hungry. He was hungry with a desperation that took his breath away. It couldn't be sated. Eating barely dulled the pain.

He felt something else, too. Along with the hunger came an inexplicable but intense desire to go to the warmlake. As the hunger churned through him, he seemed to see the bending reeds in his mind's eye, hear the clatter of their stalks and the cries and plops of the brinlins as they dropped into the water. He thought of Chalsia, his dead wife, and all the times they'd been down there together, she with her washing, him pretending to read.

He wanted to go. He wanted to walk to the edge of the water and settle into the tall, sweet grass. He wanted to lie back on the slope above the water, and surrender.

Embriem was tired. He was so very tired of fighting.

But Tassin still held on. The boy seemed nothing more than a skeleton – a network of bones with skin stretched tight over the top. He lay on the couch in the reception hall, his chest rising and falling with ragged breath.

It was time to end it. He couldn't deny this any longer. If Embriem's own suffering was this intense, he could only imagine what his son felt every time he struggled into consciousness.

Still, it was difficult. It was difficult to go into his office, to pull open his desk drawer, pick up a piece of his stationary, uncap the ink pot, and dip the fine pen his mother had given Chalsia when she'd graduated from her position as trenner and become a full scribe.

The pen almost made him change his mind. He remembered Chalsia that day, her glowing happiness. All her life, she'd been fascinated by words and letters, learning and ideas. But her parents had been poor. She'd been the oldest of several children. She was needed at home. There was no time for her to attend the cloister school.

Embriem had taught her to read. He'd done it while learning himself, the two of them sitting together on the slope above the warmlake while Chalsia's washing dried, laid out on the reeds. It had taken them years to get through the thick learning book, but it hadn't mattered. He'd treasured every moment of their time together.

Now, was he really going to do this? Was he going to kill their son? Tassin was the only piece left of the woman he had loved in this entire world.

Tears fell onto the paper, soaking into the thick pulp. Embriem wanted to throw the pen across the room, smash the ink pot on the floor. The hunger gnawed at him, clouding his mind.

Out in the hall, he heard the front door open and close. Curious, he turned towards the door. But there was no sound of footsteps, no voices.

With reluctance, he turned back to the paper. It was the right thing. Chalsia would not disagree. There was no cure for Tassin, no way out. He was suffering and would only continue to suffer. It was cowardly and selfish to delay the inevitable.

Embriem's hand was shaking. He set nib to paper and blotched the first stroke.

He didn't care. He scrawled two words, "Bring them." Then, in a hasty scramble, he signed his name.

Sitting back, he felt breathless. It was the right thing. It had to be. The church could ease Tassin's pain and deliver him, consecrated, over Tristis' threshold. Though it was a crime for one man to end the life of another, the rector could prescribe death as an act of mercy. His sisters could deliver it without pain, without fear, and with the goddess' blessing.

Embriem tossed the pen onto the desk, careless of the ink he spattered. He folded the paper, sealed it, and charged into the hall to find Baret, knowing if he waited a single second longer than necessary, he would lose courage and change his mind.

He found the servant in the back garden, weeding a bed of dewbells. Embriem hurried up to him and spoke without preamble, without explanation. "I need you to take a message to the rector at once."

As Baret set aside his dirt stained gloves, dusted off his breeches, and extended a hand for the letter, Embriem nearly snatched the paper away. He wanted to tear the sheet to shreds, return to the house, and find his son sitting up and smiling.

But that could not be. He shoved the letter into Baret's hands and turned away. He fled back towards the house, his vision obscured by fog and tears.

The fog was thick and warm and so annoying. Not even able to see the next bend in the road, Marim walked at a swift pace, her skirts growing damp as she went. The air seemed alive. She could feel the sighing touch of mist on her face, like a blind person taking the feel of her features.

Kix was delighted to be away from the house. He wheeled above her, flitting through the fog on his brilliant wings. She couldn't keep track of him in the thick air. She felt a vague worry he'd fly too high and get lost, though she knew that was impossible. Even her tessila, damaged as he was, had an uncanny ability to keep track of her.

She walked swiftly, following the slope down and down. The fog made everything silent. She thought with a curl of unease that she could pass within arm's reach of another person in this place and never know he was there.

She'd left the house in a rushing scramble, pausing only to ask Baret for directions. She reached a crossroads and picked the route that kept heading down. A few moments later, she passed a woman on the path. She was a thick figure who appeared out of the fog all in an instant. For a heart-stopping moment, Marim thought she was some massive beast. Her figure loomed, wide and formless. Sour fear spread out from Marim's belly.

Then, the fog shifted. She realized the woman was walking partially stooped, bearing a bulky bundle of reeds upon her back.

Swallowing her surprise, Marim said hello. The woman grunted in response and kept plodding up the path.

Marim continued. The high collar of her blouse grew damp and confining. She glanced around, decided she was unlikely to encounter anyone else, and unbuttoned. She folded the collar back from her scarred throat, walking a little faster.

By the time she reached the warmlake, the fog was suffocating in its warmth. The air was so thick and gray down by the water, only the change in terrain made her aware she was approaching the shore. She'd been walking on a path scored through high, dew-drenched grasses, which ended in a spit of sand. She paused, staring around, then walked ahead, taking one slow step at a time.

And finally, she saw the warmlake.

It was just a lake. She couldn't see much of it, due to the fog. The water lapped where the sand ended, little ripples catching the strange low light. Marim stooped and put her fingers in the water, then snatched them out again, startled. She'd known the warmlake would be warm. She wasn't a fool. But she'd thought warm in the sense of not cold.

This water was borderline hot. Though not anywhere hot enough to burn her, it was like the warmth of a cup of tea that has been left to sit for a quarter of an hour or so.

Marim put her hand back in the water, feeling foolish for startling herself. She heard a strange series of plunks, like pebbles dropping into the water. Then Kix gave a cry. He'd been flying up in the fog, but now he plummeted towards her and dove straight into the water. As he did so, Marim noticed the sinuous shapes beneath the surface. They were converging on her hand from every direction.

A small shriek escaped Marim as she snatched her hand out of the water again. She fell to her knees on the sand, staring down into the lake. The water was clear. She could see the mass of small bodies beneath the surface. They flowed together like a school of minnows. But they were not fish.

Marim's heart clenched with panic. She couldn't see her tessila. He had to be in there somewhere, caught in that crush of seething bodies. "Kix," she cried, knowing it was hopeless. She tried to feel for him along their bond. Some of the other Tessilari spoke of being fully aware of their tessila's every nuanced emotion, but that was not the case with Marim and Kix. She was aware of him generally. She could only feel his emotions when they were pronounced or intense or simple.

But right now, kneeling on the shore of this strange lake, she couldn't seem to feel him at all.

Was he going to drown himself? Suicide was not uncommon among the tessili who had suffered at the hands of the academy. But why now? If he'd have wanted this, he'd had plenty of opportunity on the voyage across the sea.

Marim sat very still, trying to feel what Kix was feeling, trying to pick up on any signal that his life was failing. If he died, she would die. Someone would find her body here, laid out on the sand like an abandoned puppet.

"Well," she said to herself, "at least I wouldn't have to see Embriem lose his son."

She waited, growing resigned as the moments passed. She watched the shapes underneath the water, the way they coiled and flowed around one another. They were strange creatures. About the same size as Kix, they were covered in soft scales that came in every color of the rainbow. They had narrow, sinuous bodies. If Marim hadn't known better, she'd have thought they were wingless tessili, trapped within the water by some strange spell.

The minutes dragged by. Marim didn't know how long she sat there, waiting to die. She was becoming impatient with the prospect when she heard a sound behind her – the scuff of a boot on sand.

She turned, coming to her feet in an awkward stumble. A man stood behind her, little more than an outline in the fog. He had broad shoulders and a thick head of hair, but she couldn't make out his face.

He spoke in a cautious tone. "Are you all right, miss?"

When Cockram thought of the Tessilari, he always imagined them a fierce-looking people. He envisioned the men firm, fit, and casually powerful. The women, he was certain, would be equally impressive, with tall, slender figures, piercing eyes, and enigmatic expressions.

The girl on the sand spit didn't fit his expectation. She was small, for one thing, and nothing about her carriage struck him as particularly prepossessing. His first feeling upon seeing her was one of a disappointment. This was hardly a worthy adversary.

She was kneeling by the water as he approached. He stood in the fog for a while, watching her back. She stayed there, immobile, until he came closer.

When she was kneeling, half hidden by the fog, he marked her straight back and her short hair. He felt a strange little thrill at the prospect of facing someone who could wield magics.

But when he scuffed his boot, startling her, she scrambled to her feet and spun around. As she faced him, he saw she was young and uncertain. The short haircut struck him as daring, but her eyes were wide and frightened. There was sand stuck to her skirts.

He might not have noticed her neck, except her hands flew to the throat of her blouse the moment she saw him. She made as if to raise the collar. Then, as if realizing she was drawing attention to something she wanted to hide, she stopped. Her hands fell to her sides, motionless. She seemed then to register his question. "Yes, fine. Thank you."

Cockram took a step closer, squinting through the fog. It was hard to see on a day like this, but her neck seemed scarred, the skin covered in a webbing of marred tissue. He felt a strange thrill of horror. It was as if she'd been restrained somehow, chained up by a collar around her throat. Was she a criminal, then? Did that explain her presence here? Perhaps she'd broken free of her prison and fled Masidon only to get dumped off here when Captain Tommin discovered her true nature.

Cockram took another step forward. There was a look of strain on the woman's face, a ready tension in her body. He'd heard tales: strange stories that came ashore with the sailors. He'd heard tell of female Tessilari who had been enslaved and turned into deadly assassins. Could she be one of those? She didn't look much able to kill him, but he supposed that would make her an especially effective weapon.

Cockram shifted his gaze, looking out into the fog over the warmlake. In the week since Captain Tommin's ship had put in and then left almost immediately, using the magic of its guideglobe to fight its way out of harbor against the wind and the tide, gossip of every imaginable variety had surrounded the event. There was gossip about the ship, gossip about the captain, and gossip about the young lady who had been left behind. Several people had glimpsed her walking through town alone, and others had seen her with Embriem. There were rumors she'd been sent for, rumors she was some strange, lost relation, Tassin's final hope. A healer, multiple sources confirmed, perhaps with some secret cure.

No one else seemed to guess what Cockram suspected, that the girl was a vessel for corruption. He himself could not even be sure he'd understood Captain Tommin correctly. So, he'd waited, simply letting it be known among his contacts that he'd like to be told if the newcomer ventured into town.

Now, his patience had paid off. With the girl before him at last, he could assess her for himself.

He tried to put her at ease. "It's not usually this thick, you know." He gestured at the fog, making his tone as casual as if they were old friends who'd happened to meet on the road. "The fog is always changing, as you've no doubt noted. It likes to keep us on our toes."

His friendly words had little effect. The girl's posture suggested she wanted to take another step backwards, but she could not because of the lake. When she spoke, her voice was cautious and cold. "What do you want?"

Cockram considered the question. What did he want? He wanted what he'd always wanted, which was to keep Cynnes Tarth safe, keep it pure. Delari herself knew he'd already sacrificed much to that end. Was this girl a threat? He didn't know for sure, but it seemed likely. If she had a tessila, that was one mark against her already. But one mark wasn't enough. And besides, he had no hard evidence she was anything more threatening than a foreigner.

He decided to push. Putting on his most charming smile, he looked out over the water. "I've always been very interested in the Tessilari."

The girl flinched as if he'd struck her. He'd been beginning to think he'd been wrong, that he'd misunderstood the captain's insinuations. Suppose this girl called herself a healer because she knew how to pick a few herbs and make them into a salve, or brew tea that could settle a stomach? Suppose she didn't call herself a physician because she had no proper training, but she'd needed some way to persuade the captain to take her on board his ship?

Sensing vulnerability, Cockram moved ahead one more step. He was close to the girl now, close enough he could have reached out a hand and set it on her shoulder. Could she swim? If not, there was possibility in this moment. He could take care of her right here, right now, and no one the wiser. He'd often thought the Directive a little too conservative, the process of collecting marks cumbersome and slow.

The moment seemed to stretch and lengthen. The fog surrounded the two of them, separating them from the world and its usual consequences. If only she would do or say something, reveal her true nature, he could be certain of what he must do.

But she said nothing, did nothing. She only stood there, her expression somewhat distant, as if something else occupied her attention.

There was a strange, thin cry on the heavy air. A speck of yellow appeared, flying up from the surface of the lake, streaming water. Beating brilliant wings, it flew in a spiral around Marim's body, landed on her shoulder, and hissed.

The tessila was tiny, its body no larger than Cockram's thumb. Yet as it reared back on its hind legs and skewered him with its sharp gaze, he did not doubt it would attack him if he made one false move.

Still, Cockram felt a stirring of satisfaction. There was no mistaking what she was now. This creature defined her. Aside from the wings, it was not so different from the brinlins that lived in the reeds and swam in the shallows of the warmlake: the creatures that had cost him his sister. If Adni had paid for her affinity for brinlins with her life, so too must this Tessilar die.

With her tessila's arrival, the girl revived. Color flooded back into her face. Her cheeks bloomed, giving her previous bland appearance a look of vibrancy. "You mustn't mind Kix," she said. "He's harmless."

But there was something in her tone, some underlying smugness that didn't quite fit with the words. Cockram got the sudden, uncomfortable impression she'd read his mind.

Cockram studied the creature. It gazed right back, and hissed again.

Harmless, the girl had said. Cockram very much doubted that.

CHAPTER 4

Vailria walked up the three steps to the weaver's shop. She stood in front of the closed door, taking a moment to fortify herself. It seemed the older she got, the more difficult she found basic human interaction.

Around her, the fog was all aglow. It was late afternoon: that hour when the sun's rays caught in the air, filling the entire atmosphere with a gentle luminance. She could imagine how the warmlake looked right now, with the reeds all full of dew and the water liquid gold.

For a moment, Vailria experienced an intense desire to leave. Since missing Tommin, her regular duties here in Lan Dinas seemed crushingly difficult. It would be so easy to turn around, retrace her steps, walk out past the edge of town and follow the path that led to her own little house, the forest beyond. Once home, she could sit out on the deck over the water and watch the place where the lake met the sky. At her house, she never had to deal with other people. She was in control of her own little domain.

But while Vailria was almost self-sufficient, there were some things she could not create for herself. She also had a job to do. It wouldn't do for her to cut herself off entirely from the people here. They already thought her strange. Some of them thought her a good deal worse than that. And the whole point of her being here at all was to maintain a connection, however tenuous, with these people.

So, Vailria drew in a long, slow breath and pushed her way through the door.

The weaver's shop was a vibrant place, full of bright bolts of cloth, colorful trimmings, and the scent of dyes and thread. As she entered, Vailria cast a little spell on the tiny bell that hung above the door, containing the silvery tinkle it otherwise would have made. She did it on reflex. The older Vailria got, the more noise of any kind made her uncomfortable. She stepped into the room and heard two women speaking in the low, urgent tones of gossips. "… saw Tassin on the street last week. Looked like a scarecrow, so thin, he was."

Vailria eased the door shut and drifted inside as a second speaker answered the first. "I heard his father requisitioned the butcher's boy and made him deliver a whole pile of meat up to the house every day. He all but cleared out the shop, from what I heard."

The two women were in the corner of the store, blocked from Vailria's view by a rack of imported fabrics on display. She stayed where she was, listening. Vailria wasn't above eavesdropping. In her situation, she must use the advantages she had.

There was a small silence as the two women considered the implicit contradictions in these pieces of information. There was the thump and swish of a bolt of fabric being unrolled. The first woman spoke again. "I guess, if it's the wasting disease, the poor lad doesn't have long."

"I'm not sure about the pattern on this one," the second voice said. "I think it's too bold for the drawing room. What about that other, with the blue?"

There was another pause and more soft thumps and rustling. After a moment, the second voice continued, "I knew a man who got the wasting disease. He didn't look like that boy looks. He got spots all over his skin and his hair fell out. And he got thin because he didn't eat. Couldn't keep a morsel down, poor soul." A pause, then, "Yes, this is better. Subtle. A better fit. Don't you think?"

Vailria had listened at first because it was her habit. Now her interested was piqued. But the shop owner said, "If you like this, take a look at what has newly arrived from the north isles." She began to walk towards the rack near Vailria.

Knowing she'd be seen regardless, Vailria stepped forward, moving past the rack of cloth and into the center of the shop. "Good afternoon, ladies." She said the words as if she'd just walked in, using her brightest, friendliest tone as she forced her face into a smile.

It didn't do much good. Both of the women, the shop's owner and the customer, stiffened when Vailria appeared. The shop's owner looked towards the door in surprise, as if wondering why she hadn't heard the bell. The second woman, who was running her fingers across the rich brocade of a bolt of fabric, snatched her hand back as if she'd been caught stealing biscuits. Neither of them returned the smile.

Vailria suppressed a sigh. She should be accustomed to these kinds of reactions by now. She was still a little amazed at her continued capacity to care about what these people thought of her. Nevertheless, she felt the sting of their reaction, noted the way they went from comfortable and trusting to guarded and tense.

She walked towards the till, lifting her canvas sack. "I have some weavings for you, Tashi. I'll leave them and you can add the value to my account."

Neither woman spoke as Vailria crossed the shop, winding her way around display racks and shelves piled high with fabric. She reached the table at the back of the store and set her sack on the worn counter.

The women were staring. She could feel their eyes like an itch she couldn't scratch. She turned and, unable to help herself, looked straight in their direction, daring them to keep up the scrutiny.

Both women looked away.

Vailria decided the situation was unsalvageable anyway. She might as well push. She directed her gaze towards a rack of yarn and spoke in a mild, curious tone. "I couldn't help but overhear when I came in. Embriem's son has the wasting disease?"

The customer had gone rigid. Her gaze was fixed on the fabric before her, jaw tight. The shop's owner, who was used to Vailria even if she didn't approve of her, answered in a clipped tone. "Tassin, yes. They say the physician can't help him. He eats and eats and only gets thinner for all that."

At these words, Vailria felt a shock deep within her chest. A memory from her own distant childhood flooded back. Her time with the hunger had been brief, but she'd never forgotten the way it felt, as if an endless pit had opened up inside her.

"Thank you," Vailria said. She turned her back on the two women and headed for the door.

Marim was trapped. The strange man stood on the sand, blocking her way back to shore. She was also badly shaken. Kix was with her again. He'd revealed himself to this stranger, but Marim hardly cared. He was alive, and in resoundingly high spirits. He perched on her shoulder as water dripped off his wings, preening himself. She had no idea if what he'd done was normal or not. She had no idea how he'd survived under water for so long.

She had no idea how he'd gotten out again, or why he was so excited now.

And she had no idea where this man had come from.

He was close enough now she could see him properly, even with the fog so thick. He was well-dressed in a way that suggested some effort. He wore dark trousers and a white shirt, a red vest with a brilliant green and blue scarf folded at the neck, a golden pin shaped like a rooster situated among the bright folds.

He'd gone still when Kix had appeared. Now he was staring at her tessila, something unreadable in his eyes.

Marim wished he would go. Coll wouldn't have sent her here for no reason. She felt on the verge of understanding. She needed to get a better look at the little creatures she'd glimpsed beneath the surface of the water: the brinlins. *Is it a brinlin?* This was what Tassin had said when he'd seen Kix. The boy's words should have been her first clue. Now that she thought she understood, she only hoped she wasn't too late.

A breeze stirred the fog, making it swirl. Along the shore, reeds clattered. She heard more soft cries and little plops – brinlins dropping into the water.

The man was still looking at Kix. He had blue eyes, brilliant in the glowing fog. He was not as tall as Embriem, but he was stockier, with well-muscled forearms and solid legs. He said, "What sort of powers does he give you? That tessila? I always hoped I'd see one in my lifetime." There was something a little awed in his voice.

Marim felt her attitude shift. A moment before, something in the man's eyes had scared her. Now, she realized she'd over reacted. She thought of all the times she and Kix had been overlooked, outshone as they were by even the youngest initiates at the academy.

She felt a sudden need to be modest. "Oh," she said with a nervous laugh, "Kix here isn't much of a tessila. He's not as flashy as some of the new strains. But I'm accomplished at healing, and all the basic stuff any Tessilar can do, of course." It wasn't quite true. She couldn't manage *all* the basics. But he wouldn't know how to test her on her word, even if he was inclined.

The fog swirled again. The rich afternoon light fell through the atmosphere. The man shifted as well, moving still a little closer, his expression rapt as he watched Kix shake his wings once more and fold them at his sides. He was a very nice-looking man, Marim decided. His hair was a deep, burnished red. His pale skin made his eyes look all the more blue.

"Healing." He repeated her word in a tone Marim couldn't decipher. His eyes shifted from Kix to Marim. She felt a little shock as his gaze fixed on hers. She had to consciously hold her hands at her sides to resist the urge to try to cover her scarred neck. It was too late for that. If he was going to notice, he already had. "Can you heal yourself?"

It was a strange question. Marim frowned and felt the unease return. As if sensing this, the man stepped back a pace, smoothing his silk scarf. "I don't mean to pry, my lady. My name is Cockram, proprietor of the Rooster's Comb up by the harbor." He extended a hand.

Marim hesitated. The fog swirled and shifted around them. She was struck by how alone they were: how isolated. He was much larger than she was, and Marim was no trained assassin like the girls who'd gone through the academy before her.

Cockram saw her hesitation. He smiled. The shift in his expression made him look boyish. "I'm afraid I've spooked you, following you down here like this. Only I've wanted to see a tessila for as long as I can remember. I'll leave you, my lady, but I hope we'll see each other again."

He began to withdraw his hand. Marim felt a flush of embarrassment at her suspicious reaction. She surged forward as if she'd been pushed, put her hand in his, and said, "Marim. My name is Marim, and this is Kix." She tilted her chin towards her shoulder.

Kix hissed again, unfolding his wings to flare them once more. He never liked it when people touched her.

A gust of wind hit them. The light shifted, coming up in such a bright glow Marim had to squint. For an instant, looking at Cockram's face, she thought she saw something hard come into his eyes. She'd never been much good at passive persuasion, but she began to weave a little spell, just in case.

She barely had time to get the spell started before Cockram snatched his hand out of hers as if she'd had a tack in her palm. He stepped back, blinking. The pin in his scarf seemed to catch the sunlight and throw it back in a strange flare. Marim felt her cheeks flush again, this time with shame. He couldn't have known she'd started to cast a spell, could he?

But Cockram was looking at Kix, who had begun to slink down Marim's arm, tiny fangs bared. Cockram ran a hand through his brilliant hair and managed a weak smile. "I think I'm rather more enamored with him than he is with me. I'll leave you for now, but I hope we meet again, Marim."

With that, the man turned and walked away into the glowing, swirling fog.

✛

Vailria hurried up the lane, walking as fast as she could without attracting attention. It seemed her entire life was structured around not drawing attention to herself.

Ever since she'd left the weaver's shop, a sense of urgency had been building in her. She berated herself as she went. How had she missed this? Was this not the precise reason she was here? She'd let her confusion over Tommin distract her, let herself lose sight of her real purpose.

If she lost this boy, she would never forgive herself.

The fog was restless. Tok was restless. She could feel him tucked at the base of her neck, his slim body a warm curl below her hairline. She didn't like to keep him away from the lake for more than a few hours at a time, and she'd been slow with her errands today. The longer he was out of the water, the more difficulty he had containing his energetic nature. He didn't like not being able to look around and watch what was happening. Right now, she could feel him battling a desire to inch his way to the top of her collar and peep out at the street.

He wouldn't, though. Vailria knew that. She trusted Tok more than any human. He knew it would be a disaster if his presence on her person was discovered. He'd always been intelligent, quick to grasp consequences and see outcomes. Between the two of them, she was more likely to take rash action.

The street up to Embriem's house had never felt so long. Not that Vailria had ever had much occasion to walk this way. She liked Embriem. She'd never forgotten the way he'd been as a boy: so precocious, bursting with potential but unable to focus his overabundant energy. And she'd always regretted the memory she'd had to take from him that time Chalsia's father had gotten lost in the wood.

It was one of many things Vailria had made the people of this town forget.

Now, as she hurried, she tried to prepare herself for what was to come. She would either be too late, and the boy would die before she could get him down to the lake. Or she wouldn't, and in some respects that would be even more difficult.

She thought of Embriem as she hurried. She worried it would be too much for him. He'd taken the loss of his wife hard. Vailria had heard the gossip – the talk he might have done himself harm if not for the baby.

Now, it was inevitable. Embriem would lose his son, either to death or to Vailria, which, as far as Embriem would know, was the same thing.

She reached the top of the street and slowed, composing herself to approach the large house with its long drive and imposing façade. What did two people need with all that space? Vailria's little house was warm and comfortable, with portholes in the walls of every room so Tok could come and go from the water as he pleased. Reeds grew all around the house, full of other brinlins so he was never lonely. Of the two of them, Vailria was the one who was isolated from others of her kind.

Feeling a thrill of nerves, Vailria mounted the front steps and approached the towering front doors. They were made of black walnut, composed in a pattern of panels and curves, with a set of narrow windows at either side. The knocker was a heavy black affair – a dire's head holding a ring in its mouth.

Vailria felt reluctant to touch the thing. It seemed bad luck to have such an image on the threshold of one's home.

She raised her hand towards the knocker, but the heavy door swung inward before she could touch it. A butler looked out at her, startled into silence by the sight of her, as so many of these people were.

Vailria was used to that. "Hello," she said, trying to smooth over his rude silence. She didn't know the man's name, so she hazarded on. "I'm Vailria." He would know that. Everyone in town was aware of the eccentric woman who lived at the edge of the forest. "I've come to see Embriem." She bit back the urge to explain in more detail. The less said now, the less work for her later.

The man looked discomfited, but found his voice. "I'm sorry, miss Vailria. Embriem's not well, see, and his son's worse. We're expecting the sisters from the cloister. Anyone else is to be turned away."

Vailria considered the man. She judged he didn't have a strong character. He looked nervous, standing there. She thought it wouldn't take much, just a little twist, and he'd change his mind.

But the man hadn't opened the door very wide. He was withdrawing already, easing the door closed. He was mumbling a low jumble of words. "I'm very sorry. I'll let the master know you came by." She couldn't very well lunge through the door and grab him by the wrist.

The door shut, the latch giving off a short, hard click.

Vailria felt tired. She wasn't cut out for this work, this life. Such a foolish mistake she'd made all those years ago when she'd begged to take this position. Young people, she reflected, shouldn't be allowed to make decisions about anything remotely important.

But she'd had her reasons, and anyway, there was Tommin. She would never regret their connection, no matter what it cost her to stay in this place.

Vailria stared at the dire's head for a moment. Tok was offended by this turn of events. She felt him shift within her tall collar, moving around so he was near the front and had a little sliver of a view ahead. She supposed she'd have to go around to the back of the house and find another way in.

She turned, intending to walk down the steps and make her way around the side, but gasped in surprise when she saw she was no longer alone.

A young woman stood at the base of the steps, motionless. Neither Vailria nor Tok had heard her approach, which was very strange. Between the two of them, they were hard to sneak up on.

Vailria had to resist the impulse to bark at the girl, to demand where she'd come from. But as her surprise dissipated, she caught a subtler sensation. She sensed the leftover weavings of a spell – the faint tug of magic falling away as it was let go.

Which could only mean one thing.

Vailria drew herself up a little straighter, noting the high collar on the woman's blouse, which was buttoned up around her throat. She looked her straight in the eye, trying not to show her alarm. "Who are you?" she snapped. "Where did you come from?"

✛

Marim was startled out of her thoughts when she looked up to see a strange woman standing on Embriem's doorstep. She froze in place, gazing at the woman's back, trying to decide what to do.

She'd passed the previous half hour down by the warmlake, trying to get a better look at the brinlins. Even after Cockram had left, she'd felt jumpy. She kept worrying Kix would throw himself back into the water. He didn't, though. He crawled into her collar and fell asleep.

The brinlins, Marim discovered, divided their time between swimming in the warm water and climbing about in the stands of reeds that lined the lake. The plants formed a dense screen along the lake's edge, continuous except for the occasional jut of sand. They were tall and thick and topped with silky fronds. The fronds matured into long, narrow husks not unlike those that grew on brillbane bushes.

The brinlins themselves were difficult to get a good look at. They were coy and skittish. If they were on the reeds, they tended to shift around to the other side if Marim stared at them. If they were in the water, they swam too quickly for her to lock onto. She'd spent a long while sidling up towards the reeds and standing very still, waiting until one of the little creatures got curious enough to shift back around the stem it was clinging to for a better look at her.

When, at last, one had done so, she'd been surprised. She'd expected a wingless version of Kix, but that wasn't quite right. The brinlin was similar to a tessila in shape and size, certainly, but there were marked differences. The neck was shorter and thicker, as was the tail. The legs were short, the feet webbed, and the whole body had a sinuous, slick quality. Frilled gills fluttered at the throat.

Most surprising was the coloring. All the tessili Marim had ever seen were one solid color. Not so brinlins. The particular one she got a good look at was a brilliant blue, patterned over with an array of black spots of varying size.

"What a beauty you are," she'd said. And Kix had woken up, stirred out of his sleep by a rush a jealousy. She'd backed away from the reeds, finally certain of what she needed to do.

She'd set out, walking away from the warmlake with a sense of purpose. After she'd gone a short distance, however, her skin began to prickle with nerves. The fog made it impossible to see ahead. Anyone could be there, standing just beyond her range of vision.

More to sooth herself than for any real belief she'd be bothered, Marim tried to cast a passive echo spell. It was one of the basic weavings she'd never been able to manage properly. While more accomplished casters could render themselves essentially invisible, Marim had never even succeeded in making herself forgettable. Still, she worked at it as she walked, pulling threads of magic and fiddling with them. She practiced a deviation Professor Liam had worked on with her, tailoring her magic to focus on sound in particular, since it was a sense most people relied on less than sight. She constructed what she thought might be a passable weaving, then she held it in place. She did pass a few people as she neared town—faint shapes in the fog—but she ignored them and they ignored her.

She was worrying about logistics as she reached the driveway. They'd have to get Embriem and his son down to the water as soon as possible. Hopefully Tassin wasn't too weak to make the journey. Or worse, dead. How awful would it be if Marim figured out how to help him only to deliver the news too late?

She walked through the gate, made her way up the drive, and looked up to see the woman standing on the front steps of Embriem's house. Marim was so startled by this unexpected encounter, she lost her hold on the spell she'd been playing with.

The woman, who turned as Marim stopped and made to descend the steps, went rigid when she saw she was no longer alone. She had a lean figure and a striking face and a sort of impatient confidence to her body language. There was also something a little haunted in her eyes. She reminded Marim of some of the older students she'd known at the academy – the ones who'd been forced to systematically murder others of their own kind.

Stranger than that, though, was her clothing. The woman wore a plain wool dress with a high, stiff collar concealing her throat. If this was a fashion, it was one Marim had never seen before. She resisted the urge to touch her own scarred neck. She'd raised her collar again and buttoned it on her way back from the lake.

Seeing her, the woman spoke. "Who are you?" She sounded angry. "Where did you come from?"

Marim blinked, staring at the closed door of the house and thinking about the urgency of the situation. She felt Kix wake up, roused by Marim's racing emotions. Although in the academy

Marim had learned to avoid confrontation whenever possible, now she didn't have much choice. Tassin would die if she didn't get past this woman and into the house. "I'm sorry. I'm needed inside." Her voice, much to her dismay, came out thin and low.

The woman started down the steps. Marim felt a thrill of real fear – far more potent than the discomfort she'd felt when she faced Cockram. She was filled with a conviction this woman wanted to do her harm.

The woman reached the bottom of the steps and extended her hand. "I'm Vailria." Her tones was less brittle now, but still there was that sharpness in her eyes. "I've known Embriem since he was a boy."

Marim looked at the hand. It was well kept, with smooth nails and a fine webbing of wrinkles showing across the knuckles. It was hard to guess the woman's age. At least 40, Marim thought. Maybe older.

The woman's face softened as Marim hesitated. She began to look less severe, almost friendly. But Marim's encounter with Cockram had spooked her. She thought of the way he'd reacted to her touch, the strange way his rooster pin had caught the light and flared.

She did not put her hand in the woman's hand. She raised her skirts and dipped a tiny curtsey. "I'm Marim. I'm needed inside."

She was about to dodge around the woman, to run past her if need be, when Vailria's face changed. All the color drained out of her cheeks as her eyes locked onto something in the distance.

Unable to help herself, Marim turned to look.

She saw a string of figures, mere shadows off in the fog. With them came the slow tread of feet, and the sad toll of the death bell.

Embriem was out of tears. His eyes felt hollowed out and dry. His head thrummed with a dull ache. His stomach was a living thing with claws and teeth and a desire to rip him to shreds from the inside. But he no longer associated the hunger with a need to eat. He was done with that. Embriem was done with everything.

Baret had returned, bearing a reply from the rector. The man would come, leading a procession of solemn sisters. They would bring the death serum – a potent potion whose secret was known only to the senior physician at the cloister. The sisters would gather around Tassin. They would sing a hymn of love and mourning. The rector would speak and light a candle. Then, the physician would unseal a tiny jar. She would dip a silver wand into the sticky serum, and wipe the wand along the boy's lips. She would do this three times. Then she would withdraw, to dispose of the remainder of the deadly concoction.

Tassin's breathing would slow. The toxin would work its way into his system. Within a few minutes, his heart would stop. He would pass peacefully. No more pain. No more hunger.

Embriem would be free at last. He would see the sisters and the rector out of his home. He would wait long enough so he did not risk catching them up on the road. He would find the fine, sharp dagger his father had given him for his seventh birthday and strap it to his belt. Then he would walk to the warmlake, sit down in the reeds, and open his wrists. His death would not be as painless as his son's, but Embriem didn't mind. He would settle back in the grass and think about Chalsia until his thoughts stilled to nothing.

The distant, heavy click of the front door opening startled Embriem out of his thoughts. He sat up, blinking. He'd been so wrapped in his vision for what was to come, he'd all but convinced himself it was done already. Now he heard the murmur of voices, the soft tread of many feet, the sweet, solemn toll of the death bell.

The sisters had arrived.

CHAPTER 5

Vailria made a frantic gesture, indicating Marim should follow. She turned and strode a short distance away from the steps. Together, they watched the procession that passed like a string of ghosts in the fog. The rector was in the lead, wearing the red robes of his station and holding the bell on its pole. The sisters drifted after, wearing black and walking in twos. There were six of them. They moved at a steady pace, heads bowed, hands folded in their sleeves, murmuring a prayer as they went. The seventh came behind, wearing white. "They have come for Tassin," Vailria said. "To release him from life with Delari's blessing."

Marim stared in shock. Embriem had mentioned something about this, a tradition here on the island of letting the sick depart their suffering.

"No." The word slipped out of Marim in a hoarse whisper. She stared at the procession, heart hammering. Why were they here? Surely Embriem hadn't given up the fight? What was the use of Marim keeping Tassin alive for so long only to be killed?

Angry, fearful, helpless, Marim stared in silent horror as the procession reached the house. She had to stop this, but how? She was only one person. True, she was Tessilari. But she was weak. How she wished now for the company of her more talented friends – the friends who had always made her feel useless by virtue of the magic they could wield without effort, without thought or struggle or care.

"What are your talents?" The question came in a quick, low voice. Marim turned. The woman in the strange dress stood a few paces away in the fog, staring at the sisters, eyes glittering with hate.

"What?" After so many days filled with nothing, days that had dragged by at a snail's pace, Marim felt as if time had bolted and was now careening at full tilt, with no thought for her safety. She remembered the way she'd used to run down the steep slope behind the academy with the other students, letting her momentum carry her until she couldn't have stopped if she'd tried. There would be that moment: the reckless thrill. Then she'd hit the water of the slow, deep river with a splash and a shriek. She'd go under, the cool water closing around her. She'd hold her breath and come up laughing as her friends plunged in around her. They would tread water, panting, the spice of the river sharp on their tongues as their tessili wheeled on the blue air overhead.

"I don't know who you are or why you're here, but I judge by the look on your face you don't want this to happen." The woman gestured towards the sisters filing through the front door, moving as implacably as the sun. "I don't either, but the cloister has authority I can't override. So, I will ask again. What can you do?"

Marim heard a small sob escape her. Kix, spurred by her emotional turmoil, clawed his way out of her collar. She was too distracted to contain him. Before she quite knew what was happening, he was in the air, wheeling around her head in restless flight.

Vailria went very still. Her eyes tracked Kix. For the first time, her face was free of anger. Kix settled on Marim's shoulder, wings outstretched. The woman's eyes filled with a kind of awe.

Marim heard a hiss. A small movement near the woman's collar caught her eye.

Vailria's face changed. The hardness came back, the lips firmed with determination. She brought a hand to her throat as if adjusting her collar, deftly blocking Marim's view.

But it was too late. Marim had seen. She'd seen the brinlin's blunt-nosed head, its glittering black eyes and fluttering gills, a pattern of red dots thrown across a purple hide.

Marim felt a surge of conflicting emotions, a combination of hope and fear all mixed with the desperate sense of urgency. "So I'm not the only one on the island who knows what's happening."

Vailria's eyes gave nothing away. She gestured towards the procession again. The last of the sisters were walking through the door. "They know also. Or at least, they know some shred of the truth. It's why they're here."

"I have no particular talents," Marim said. Her voice came out in a thin quaver. She felt small and useless against the events unfolding around her. Vailria's eyes were sharp and perceptive. She said nothing, and Marim tried to explain. "Kix is … he … we … nearly died when we were young. It was just before the Tessilari rose again. We were …." She trailed off. It was impossible to explain in concise terms. "Anyway, Kix isn't quite right. He's simple. Mentally, I mean."

Vailria was still looking at Kix. She answered in a matter of fact tone, as if what Marim had said was to be expected. "I'm strong in the mental arts. I can change people's minds, alter memories, and I'm good with illusions. But I'm sure you know the limitations. I have to be touching someone to reliably influence his thoughts. Illusions are limited in their usefulness."

"Illusions," Marim echoed. She'd never heard of a Tessilar with such a skill. She stared at Vailria's collar, hoping for another glimpse of the brinlin.

"No one in town knows what I am." Vailria said this in the same, businesslike tone. "It's very important they not find out."

"But they'll both die." Marim gestured towards the great shape of the looming house. "If we don't get them to the lake, they will die. What usually happens to people here who get the hunger?"

Vailria frowned, her mouth a thin, straight line. "Both of them? Embriem?" She sounded surprised.

Marim nodded, and Vailria closed her eyes for a moment, releasing a breath. Was that relief on her face?

Marim frowned, looking at the other woman. "So the sisters, are they acting out of malice? Is it the same way here as it used to be in Masidon? You are hunted and reviled?"

Vailria shook her head. "It is not that simple. No. The rector believes this an act of compassion. Or at least, he forces himself to believe that. He thinks death is the only way to redeem him."

Marim was keenly aware of time ticking away as they spoke. She felt a pull to go to the house, to find Embriem, to tell him what she'd discovered. "So we explain," Marim said. "Once people understand …"

Vailria cut her off, her voice coming out in a snarl. "Once they understand, they will kill me as well as the boy and his father, and perhaps you for good measure. This isn't Deramor, girl. We have no royal decree to protect us. All people fear and hate what is different, what is beyond their control."

Marim felt a chill settle over her heart. She understood what Vailria faced. Even in Deramor, the years since the Tessilari had come out of hiding had been far from smooth. There had been incidents and confrontations, many of them violent. One night an angry mob had appeared at the gates of the academy. "It'll be a work in progress, this peace," Professor Liam had said. "And it won't be settled during our lifetimes. Or," he'd amended, looking at her with grave eyes, "during mine, anyway."

Again, Marim felt a sense of urgency. Where were the sisters now? In the drawing room? Beginning the final prayer? She looked away from Vailria, taking a small step towards the looming house. "Well, none of this matters right now. We have to get Tassin out of there."

Vailria nodded. "Yes," she said. "I will need your help. The final prayer and blessing take about twenty minutes. That is our window to act."

✢

The sisters were in the drawing room, gathered in a small knot near the door. They were murmuring in low voices, preparing the salve. Embriem heard the pop of a seal being released.

The rector stood with him, his lean face drawn with regret. He set a hand on Embriem's shoulder and Embriem had to resist the fierce desire to shrug it off, to push the man away from him, to gather his son in his arms and run for the door.

He did none of these things. He only stood. Helpless.

The rector spoke. "I must lead the prayer." His red robes were plain but made of rich cloth. The wide sleeve swayed as he dropped his hand and turned, walking to where the sisters waited.

It was the most counter-intuitive thing in the world, Embriem thought, to stand by and watch someone kill your child. Had

Chalsia been there, would she have allowed this? Or would she have fought tooth and nail, never giving up?

Embriem turned towards his son. As the rector lit a beeswax taper and the sisters lined up to light their own candles from his, Embriem looked down at the couch where his boy lay. Tassin's eyes were closed, his long lashes pale against cheeks. Other than those lashes and that familiar tumble of hair, the boy was unrecognizable. He lay sunken in his clothing, taking up no more space than a skeleton. Only the feeble rise and fall of his chest indicated he still lived.

Embriem could remember a time when those limbs had been soft with baby fat. They'd grown from short and chubby into the sturdy legs of a healthy boy. He couldn't believe now this slip of a wasted child was his son, his own lively Tassin.

Embriem felt a touch on his ankle. He started in place, looking down with confusion. Crouching by his feet, hidden from the rest of the room by the couch, was Marim.

Annoyance and confusion mingled in Embriem. Behind him, candles lit, one by one. He almost snapped at the girl, almost told her to get up, to get out of his room, out of his house. He never should have brought her back from the ship, never should have trusted her. She had said she was helping Tassin when really she'd only prolonged his suffering.

But her hand was on his ankle. She was speaking in a low, urgent voice. "Embriem." Her words carried no further than his ears. "We have to go. This doesn't have to happen. Tassin does not have to die. All we need to do is go to the warmlake."

Warmlake. The word reached Embriem's ears and lit that latent desire, the impulse he'd been fighting all day. He did want to go to the warmlake. He would. He would go to the warmlake as soon as his son was free, released from pain and delivered into Delari's arms.

The sisters were turning now, lit candles held aloft. One last figure, this one wearing white, held the serum and the wand. The black clad sisters formed behind the rector, two by two, the sister in white at the back. They would cross the room now, begin their prayer. They would form a circle around Tassin's couch. They would call down Delari's blessing and administer the serum.

Marim's hand on his ankle began to move. At first he didn't understand what she was doing, but gradually he realized she was groping up his trouser leg, fingers searching for the top of his sock. He was about to pull away, to snap at her, to tell her to go, but she was still speaking in that urgent whisper and his mind seemed all a jumble, full of conflict. He remembered his wife, dying because the physician could not stop the bleeding that had begun with Tassin's birth. He remembered her pale lips and her cold hands and what she had said. "Take care of our boy, Embriem. I love you. Take care of him."

Embriem's eyes were full of tears. The pinpoints of candlelight were smeared sparks of light. Marim was talking, but her words made no sense. "What you see on the couch isn't Tassin anymore.

It's an illusion. Vailria has your son. She came in and took him, hiding herself in a cloak that's woven with a passive echo spell. She's already gone. She's waiting outside the door. We have to get Tassin to the warmlake. You have to come as well. Now. Before they realize what's going on. You have to come."

As Marim spoke these final words, Embriem felt her fingers come into contact with the skin of his leg. A sudden warmth bloomed through him, accompanied by a jolt of certainty. He blinked, looking at Tassin. He could see now the boy didn't look quite right. There was a thinness to his form, a quality of unreality Embriem hadn't noticed before.

The rector was a few feet away, leading his sisters, chanting in a monotone. Marim's face was pale. Sweat had beaded on her brow. "Go," she said. "Get out of here. Say you can't stand it. Leave."

Embriem blinked, turned, and faced the rector, who had stopped by the foot of the couch. "Delari forgive me," he blurted in a choked voice. "I cannot stand here and watch my son die."

The fog was heavy, dense, and alive. Cockram had seen it like this before. It was the season for storms. They were ponderous, slow moving systems that could settle over the island for days. The clouds would loom, blotting out the sun and filling the air with reckless lightning. The fog would boil, sometimes maturing to rain, sometimes hanging so thick Cockram would get soaked just walking across the yard. During the worst storms, the ocean would grow restless and high, sometimes thrashing over the seawall to lash at the warehouses and wharves. Once or twice, the waves had reached far enough inland even to damage the Rooster's Comb.

The conditions suited Cockram's mood. He stood at the top of Embriem's driveway, staring after the procession of sisters. He'd followed them from the cloister, listening to the tolling death bell, feeling his heart throb with pain and hate and despair. Memories rose up in him, memories of another day he'd gone to the cloister and asked to speak to the rector. Once there, he'd betrayed the secret his sister had made him swear to keep.

Cockram had been a boy then, nervous and unsure. The rector had received him with warmth, listening to his story with great attention. When Cockram was done, the rector spoke at length. It was a blessing, he said, that there were people like Cockram in this world – people who were bigger, stronger, more insightful than the common man, people who could recognize the importance of working for the greater good. People like Cockram could be trusted with secrets – great secrets only a few people knew.

The rector had explained about the marks, then, and the final test.

Waiting in the fog, Cockram adjusted his scarf, smoothing the knot and trying to push the memories from his mind. He didn't regret what he'd done. Regret would imply he'd acted in error.

Even now, he knew he'd done the right thing. When he understood, the rector had told him what to do. A few days later, Adni failed the test of the ring. That made three marks for her.

Three marks was the limit.

Cockram had been the one to test Adni. She'd failed at once, taking the ring Cockram offered her only to drop it instantly, a look of shock on her face. She'd sat down, hard, then, collapsing onto the floor as if he'd clubbed her in the head.

Cockram had understood what it meant. He picked the ring up from where it had rolled and clinked against the wall of her little bedroom. It sparked against his palm when he touched it, so he put in his pocket, fast.

Leaving his sister sitting stunned, he'd walked back to the cloister. The rector had been waiting, praising him, taking the ring back. He'd shown Cockram his list, let him read the Directive one more time.

Then he'd given Cockram a potion. "Put two drops in your sister's tea, once a day. Make sure no one sees you."

When Cockram had hesitated, Dinon explained. "Sometimes, the gods must act through men. Very special men. Like you."

No, Cockram did not regret what he'd done. What he regretted was that he'd been forced to act in the first place.

The minutes ticked by, the sky darkening. A distant rumble of thunder made the air shudder. Cockram stared towards the house, able to make out the smudge of lit windows through the fog. He looked at his pocket watch, squinting to make out the hands. It had been twenty minutes since the procession had gone in. It must be almost over by now.

The fog shifted again. Cockram's ears caught a sound. He straightened, staring. He made out footsteps approaching quickly, and someone's fast breath. A shape started out of the gloom, details filling in as it drew near.

It was Marim, all but running up the drive. She carried something in her arms, a small body bundled up against her chest.

At first, Cockram could only gape in disbelief. Marim moved easily, not appearing in the least encumbered by her burden. It was impossible. Surely it was not Tassin she carried?

Before Cockram could think or act, she was gone, hurrying past in the fog. She never saw him, but as she swept by, Cockram got a good look at what lay in her arms. He saw the pale face, the closed eyes, the emaciated arms folded on the chest.

It was Tassin. There couldn't be any doubt.

Frozen with confusion, Cockram stood in place. The sound of Marim's footsteps faded to nothing. He stared towards the house, expecting to hear an outcry, a jumble of raised voices, perhaps a sister or two running in pursuit.

But there was no alarm, no sound or movement at all. For a moment, Cockram felt so disoriented he thought he must have imagined her.

Then, all in a rush, he understood. He murmured the answer under his breath. "She's bewitched them. She's got them under her spell."

Cockram stepped onto the lane, moving now with a renewed sense of purpose. He began to jog, moving in the direction Marim had gone. The rector's words came back to him, ringing in his ears all these years later. *It's a blessing there are people like you in the world. People who can be counted on to do the right thing, no matter how difficult.*

Cockram had done the right thing all those years before. He'd put the drops in his sister's tea, as instructed. He'd watched her fall ill, watched her begin to waste away. He'd watched the physician come and go, confused, helpless, without answers. At last, he'd stood with his mother and father, tears streaming down his face as the death bell rang at their door.

Tassin was marked, a vessel of corruption, like Adni had been all those years go. Cockram had done the right thing once. He'd simply have to do it again.

CHAPTER 6

Marim walked through the restless fog, her mind full of contradictory thoughts. She was excited and Kix was agitated, made frantic by her emotional high.

The escape from Embriem's house had been close. Too close. Marim had never pushed so hard, never drawn so heavily on her bond with her tessila. She'd thought she would fail and Embriem would refuse to leave. The rector would find her hiding behind the couch, the fact Tassin's body was an illusion would be discovered before they were all safely away.

But those things hadn't happened. At the very last moment, Marim's passive persuasion spell had worked. Embriem had lit from the room like a startled rabbit. She'd taken two deep breaths and sidled to the wall to creep along in the shadows. It helped the sky was growing dark and the only light in the dim room came from the candles. It helped the sisters and the rector were all staring after Embriem as he barged out. They never saw Marim. She slipped out a different door, hurried down two long hallways, and met Vailria. Embriem was with her by then, gazing with confusion at Tassin, who lay propped against the wall.

Vailria glanced at Marim and gave a curt nod. "Take the boy."

There was no arguing with that tone. Marim knelt and scooped young Tassin into her arms. He was not as heavy as a five-year-old boy should have been, but he also was not light. She cast a passive bearing spell so she could carry him with almost no effort. "Embriem," she said, "it's time to go."

But Embriem only stood, gazing blankly at the tile floor where his son had been sitting. Marim took a step towards the door, but he made no move to follow.

Vailria made an impatient gesture, her face as stern and sharp as ever. "Go, Marim. There's no time left for that boy. We'll catch up."

Marim glanced at Embriem, expecting him to object, but his face had gone oddly and smooth, as if he wasn't hearing them speak.

So Marim was on her way, hurrying down the cobbled lane with Tassin in her arms. The air was alive around her, dense and roiling. Thunder growled in the distance. The very air seemed to tremble and quake.

The houses she passed were mere outlines in the gloom. Her high emotions carried her, but beneath the pounding of her heart and the sense of urgency, Marim felt a growing fatigue. Kix, currently wheeling on the troubled air in high spirits, would be exhausted tomorrow. He'd probably go through the stitchring and sleep for an entire day.

Marim was nearing the place where the lane that led to Embriem's house met the town's main thoroughfare when she heard the slap of hurrying feet behind her. At first, she was not alarmed. Vailria and Embriem should be joining her any minute now.

The footfalls approached and slowed. Marim turned to see a single figure, a man, faceless in the fog. An unpleasant bolt of shock shot through her. This was neither Embriem nor Vailria. It was Cockram.

This was such an unpleasant surprise, Marim lost her grip on her passive bearing spell. Tassin's weight came onto her suddenly, making her stagger. She grimaced, gritted her teeth, and refocused. The boy's body became light again. But now that undercurrent of fatigue she'd been feeling was deeper, more urgent, difficult to ignore.

Cockram's steady voice sounded out of the gloom. "Is that Marim? Marim of the Tessilari?" There was a note of contrived innocence in his tone that made Marim think he'd been lying in wait for her.

But how? How could Cockram have guessed she'd be coming this way?

She didn't answer his question. She wasn't trying to be rude, but she had no attention to spare for conversation. Kix was beginning to feel his fatigue. He flew down out of the restless sky and settled on her shoulder, where he sat glaring at Cockram.

The man caught up and fell in step next to Marim, matching his stride to hers. He walked with her for a time, staring at the boy in her arms. "I don't mean to pry." His voice still had that theatrical quality, like an actor overplaying his roll, "But does Embriem know you have his son?"

It was a reasonable enough question, Marim supposed. She was a stranger here. Cockram was not. He'd have heard all sorts of lurid stories about the Tessilari, some of them probably featuring harmless-seeming young women who kidnapped helpless children during strange storms.

Still, it was annoying. Cockram gave no explanation for his presence on this street. He didn't apologize for running out of the mist that way and startling her. Worse, she had no easy way to get rid of him. Annoyance swirled through her, causing her to lose her hold on her spell again. She had to stop for a moment and shift Tassin in her arms. He moaned as she adjusted him, but did not wake. As far as she knew, the boy hadn't woken at all today. She worried it was too late, that he wouldn't return to consciousness on the lake shore. If he couldn't wake up, she didn't think he could bond with a brinlin.

Marim, determined not to distract herself with things she could worry about later, tried to weave her spell again. But she couldn't get a grip on the magic. She could feel it there, just on the other side of her bond with Kix. But when she reached for it, it seemed to slide away, like beads of mercury slithering out of reach.

She paused, gathered Tassin closer to her chest, and continued on. He wasn't so heavy she couldn't carry him without the spell.

Cockram continued next to her, his broad forehead creased with concern. He spoke again, voice hesitant. "I've known Embriem since he was a boy, see. My wife was his wife's aunt's cousin, which makes me Tassin's great uncle, or something."

They reached the town. As far as Marim could tell, the street was deserted. The fog around her was aglow with the light from many windows, but she saw no movement as she turned left and hurried for the path on the other side of the row of shops, the one she knew led to the warmlake.

As Marim turned, Cockram did as well. She realized the man was not going to leave her alone, not until she gave him some kind of reassurance. She sighed. Her arms were growing fatigued. Tassin was a dead weight in her arms, limp and leaden. She spoke, unable to keep her annoyance out of her tone. "Embriem will be catching up with us any moment."

They hurried through the town, past one bright window after another. On the other side, the air seemed all the darker as the light fell behind. Marim reached the path that left the main thoroughfare, continuing down towards the warmlake. She turned onto it, trying again to gather the magic for the passive bearing spell.

She almost had it. She could feel the magic there, tantalizing with its nearness. She was focused inward, intent on her spell. She was so distracted, she tripped on a hump in the trail and stumbled so hard, she fell to her knees.

Pain lanced through her legs. Her mouth snapped shut and she bit her tongue. She struggled and barely caught her balance in time to save herself tumbling forward on top of Tassin.

Shaken, even a little dazed, Marim knelt in the fog. There was a movement beside her. She looked up to see Cockram standing over her, his handsome face creased with sympathy. He spoke, his voice throbbing with concern. "Can I help in some way? Carry the boy, perhaps?"

✛

From her position in the hall outside the drawing room, Vailria listened to the death prayer. The strain of holding the illusion was beginning to mount. As she concentrated on her work, the rhythm of the chant caused a slow boil of hatred to build inside her.

For the most part, Vailria did not let the anger overtake her. For the most part, she forgave these people their ignorance and their vile lack of understanding. She was able to live on the fringe of their sad little society, doing her part to protect the forest and what lay hidden within. She couldn't even entirely hold it against them, what they were doing now. Tassin *was* suffering. If there hadn't been a way to save his life, helping him die would have been a kindness.

But there was a way to save his life. And while Vailria was certain the sisters did not know about this, she was also confident someone in the church, someone powerful, did.

Which meant this ceremony was sanctioned, deliberate, murder.

Or at least, it would have been had Vailria not intervened. Tassin was safe, even now being carried away by Marim. Vailria was holding the illusion of the boy in place, making everyone in the room believe he still lay on his couch, buying as much time as she could.

They were close to the end of the prayer now. Vailria recognized the shift in the chant that meant it had entered its final phase. She put a hand on Embriem's arm. The man had been standing near her, dazed. Passive persuasion, when clumsily done, had that effect sometimes. In the aftermath of the spell, it stole a person's ability to act without guidance for a short while. He'd watched Marim leave with his son, encased in this strange, passive stillness.

Vailria nodded towards the entryway and mouthed the words, "It's time to go."

Embriem wavered, still stuck. Vailria had no time to reassure him. She concentrated, pouring as much magic as she could into the illusion in the other room. Then she cut ties with it, severing it from herself. It would lose coherence gradually now, fading to nothing within five to ten minutes.

At which point, the jig would be up. Unless someone tried to touch it before then, and realized it was not solid.

There was no time for delay. Vailria headed for the exit, steering Embriem with a firm hand. The man moved woodenly. She had to remind herself he had just been subjected to a spell, and he was well into the hunger himself – a crucial detail she'd been unaware of until the Tessilari girl had mentioned it. His arm felt taut and wiry beneath her fingers and his face was creased with pain and sorrow.

They moved together through the silent house, reached the front door, and stepped into the thick air outside. As they moved up the drive, Embriem gained momentum, shouldering off the after effects of Marim's spell. Vailria let her hand fall away. A moment later, the man spoke. "I don't understand why you're doing this. What makes you think you can help? How will we explain when they realize Tassin is gone?"

Vailria did not look at Embriem. She walked at a steady pace, taking comfort from Tok's soft presence against her neck. It would not be easy to convince Embriem of what had to come next. He was an important man on this island, with family and wealth and a business to run. Nevertheless, Vailria was relieved to know she would not, after all, have to separate him and his son. She would take them both. Embriem would resist, but persuasion was one of

Vailria's strongest talents. That was why she'd been given the
position here in the first place.

Right now, Embriem was too scattered and confused to be
worth talking to. The fog was wet, almost to the thickness of rain.
Vailria pulled her hood up and began to walk faster. "We'll talk
when you and your son are both feeling better. For now, we have
no time to waste. Tassin's life is at stake, and yours is also. We
must hurry."

They walked in silence until they reached town. The high
street was deserted. They moved on as the air continued to
thicken, flickering now with restless lightning.

Embriem was pulling himself together. He'd been walking
next to her with his long, even steps, but now he suddenly stopped
short to stare at her with an expression of pure shock. Vailria
stopped as well, watching as realization dawned in his face.

"It's the brinlin, isn't it? Marim said Tassin needed a tessila to
bond with, but that's wrong. What he needs is a brinlin. You must
have one too. Which means you can … you are …"

Watching Embriem struggle, Vailria felt a small surge of guilt.
He'd seen Tok once, long ago, along with many other things.

She'd taken those memories from him. It was what she did.
But if she hadn't, his son would never have come so close to death.

Vailria spoke in a cool, crisp tone. "Embriem," she said. "I'll
explain everything later. Right now, there is no time."

She turned and began to walk again. She'd taken only a few
steps when she felt the air come alive around her. A great ripple of

magic passed over her, snaking across her skin with prickling intensity.

She stopped, gasping and confused. It took her mind a moment to light on the only possible explanation. "Marim," she whispered.

Vailria began to run.

Cockram was many things, but a murderer was not one of them. He was a good man, a good husband, a good father. He'd spent his whole life contributing to the community here on Cynnes Tarth, and it was his sense of responsibility that drove him now.

He'd come to a critical moment. He supposed if he was a different kind of man, a man violence came more naturally too, he could have done away with Marim in a straightforward matter. If he said he caught her trying to kidnap Tassin, said she attacked him when he questioned her, no one would challenge his story. No one would suggest he'd done anything other than what was right.

Marim was taking Tassin to the warmlake, and she had to be stopped. What would have to happen would only be harder, more traumatic for everyone, if Tassin recovered from the hunger.

Still, the thought of violently attacking a helpless woman who doubtless didn't think she was doing anything wrong was more than Cockram could quite bring himself to do. So he considered his options as he kept pace with her, watching her closely. There was something wrong with her, he decided. She didn't appear to be injured, but as he followed her through town and onto the path that led to the warmlake, she walked as if the weight of the emaciated child was too much for her to bear. He supposed it was too much to hope she would simply collapse of her own volition. If she made it all the way to the lake, he could drown her. But he couldn't let her carry the boy that far.

In the case of Cockram's wife, it had been easy. As soon as he'd caught wind she was cheating on him with a trader from a nearby island—a man who Cockram had welcomed in his own establishment time and time again—Cockram had begun making plans. It all came together so nicely. The next time the trader appeared, he sat late at the bar, as was his habit. Cockram's wife sweetly suggested her husband might go up to bed, as she often did when the common room was down to one or two patrons. Cockram kissed her, then magnanimously poured her and the trader a fine brandy before saying good night.

The brandy was drugged. He got into bed, pretending to sleep. He heard his wife come up to check on him, then leave again. When he heard her lock up downstairs and slip out the back, he followed. She hurried through the foggy night to the trader's small barge. Cockram stood on shore, shivering, and waited for all on board to go quiet.

After that, it was child's play to unslip the oars and set a small fire on the prow. As Cockram untethered the vessel from the dock, he felt a sense of pride. He was not a man who took his problems to the town hall, sapping resources and making a mockery of his family name. He was not a murderer. He was someone who delivered justice.

He'd given the barge a firm push and watched it dissolve into the fog.

The situation now was trickier. He hadn't had time to prepare. He kept pace with the girl as she made her way nearer and nearer to the warmlake. He was beginning to think he would have to intervene directly, no matter how distasteful that might be, when Marim tripped and fell to her knees.

While planning and strategy were Cockram's strengths, he wasn't half bad at improvisation. Feigning concern, he offered his help. Then he waited as Marim seemed to consider. At last, she nodded and sat back, prepared to hand over the boy.

Crouching in the damp grass, Cockram collected Tassin into his own arms. He felt a momentary shock at the scant weight of the child, the sharp jut of elbows and hips. He snugged the boy against his chest and stood, looking down at Marim. She gazed up, dazed. Her voice came out thin and wobbly, but infused with a note of urgency. "Take him to the warmlake. He must get to the shore, near the reeds. Hurry."

Cockram should have left it there. In the months that followed, with everything that was to come, he would regret this moment. It would have been so easy. The fog was thick and dark, the air heavy. All he would have had to do was turn around, take the boy, carry him away. He could have set out as if doing what she asked. Once out of Marim's sight, he could have taken Tassin anywhere, done nothing, and the boy would have died.

Instead, he looked at Marim. He thought about the scars he'd seen on her neck. He wondered what crimes a person would need to commit to end up so marked. He knew, intuitively, she would cause trouble for him if he left her here now. She knew too much, was bent on interfering. The rector would have to keep an eye on her, tally the marks up until he could act. By then, who knows how much damage she'd have done?

She was not a large person. Her neck was so slender. It wouldn't be difficult, he thought, to deal with her here and now. She was so out of it already, maybe she wouldn't even fight.

Cockram walked a short distance away, stooped again and set the boy in the grass. He was gentle: as gentle as he'd been with his own daughter when she'd been small and he'd lifted her in and out of her crib. It wasn't the boy's fault, what was happening to him, any more than it had been Adni's fault.

Marim, still kneeling, looked up as Cockram returned, an expression of confusion on her face. As he reached out and gently set his strong hands around her slender neck, he saw realization and fear flash through her eyes. She recoiled from him, trying to push herself to her feet.

But it was too late. Cockram's large, strong hands closed about her throat, and he began to squeeze.

There was something wrong. It wasn't to do with Tassin, who was so weak now he barely responded even when Marim almost dropped him. It wasn't to do with Cockram, who was behaving very strangely indeed. It was something to do with Marim herself, and her bond with Kix. She felt as if the world had become thin – her presence in it somehow tenuous.

After she fell to her knees, she saw she could go no further. She accepted Cockram's offer of help, and felt him ease the boy's narrow body out of her arms. Unburdened, she felt a surge of relief. It didn't matter who took the boy to the warmlake as long as he got there very soon.

As Cockram walked off to follow her instructions, Marim closed her eyes and tried to recover her senses. Kix was unusually far away from her. She could feel him. He was flying high in the foggy sky, pursuing some purpose she couldn't decipher. She knelt on the narrow path, feeling the damp seep into her skirts. She was certain she'd never been so tired. Even at the academy, she'd never managed so many spells in one day, certainly not so many effective spells.

She supposed it was over-extension. She'd seen other students at the academy turn woozy and dazed when they pushed themselves too hard or too long. The condition could be fatal. Certainly at the academy it was taken seriously. Those affected were rushed to the infirmary and attended around the clock by at least one healer.

Out here, in the fog, Marim was alone. She comforted herself with knowing, if she died, she'd have done so helping someone. If Tassin lived, the people here would have to learn from his experience. They'd see the brinlin for what they were. They would celebrate the great gift they'd had in their very midst all this time. It wasn't such a terrible thing to die for. And really, hadn't Marim thought, many times, death wouldn't be such a horrible thing?

She heard the soft thump of a boot on earth.

Confused, she looked up. Cockram was still there, standing over her. And where was Tassin? She couldn't see him. Marim felt her mind bend with confusion. How long had she been kneeling here? Had Cockram already gone to the warmlake? Was he returning now, to carry her as well?

Looking up, Marim saw a strange glint against his neck scarf, a wink of light on gold. A thought sprang into her head. *He's come back. He's come back, and he's going to kill me.*

Marim tasted sour fear. She strained to see through the fog. Though Cockram's features were dim in the fuzzy air, there was no mistaking his hard expression. For a moment, his face seemed to blur into another face – the face of a man she remembered all too well. Nylan, the handler who could have, would have, killed her.

Terrified, Marim meant to scramble to her feet. But it was no good. Her body was heavy, her mind dull. As she felt Cockram's hands close about her throat, she wondered if he could feel her scars through the thin fabric of her blouse.

She didn't struggle. She was too weak to shake him off, too tired to fight. She couldn't breathe. Gray spots were blooming over her vision. She closed her eyes, giving in. She didn't know why this man was trying to kill her, but it didn't matter now.

She felt Kix before she heard him, felt his attention snap back from the vague state of mind that had led him to fly so high into the stormy sky.

Marim's tessila noticed her predicament. He was confused by it at first, but when he realized what was happening, a great bloom of rage ripped through his psyche.

At the academy, Marim had heard many people say there was a mismatch between the tiny size of the tessili and the huge emotions they felt. This had been one of the theories put forth by one of the professors as to why Kix couldn't shift. Whatever had happened to him, whatever had broken in his head or his soul when he and Marim almost died, his feelings were muted. He felt things, but not the way other tessili did. Even when angry, he was easily distracted. He would flit from one emotion to the next like a butterfly sampling blooms.

Now, Marim was dying. She was not only dying, she was being murdered. This was enough to fill even Kix with focused rage.

As her eyes filled with blackness and her ears began to pound, Marim lost track of everything except Kix and his building feeling of towering rage.

Kix was coming, and he was incensed. Marim had never picked up on such a distinct emotion from her tessila before. It rippled through her, pushing back some of the fog in her mind. She began to struggle, heaving against Cockram's hands with a great surge. His grip slipped enough she was able to suck in one shallow breath.

She heard Cockram swear, felt the hands clamp down again.

As he did, Kix reached them. The tiny tessila plunged out of the shifting fog and threw himself at Cockram's face to claw furiously at the man's right eye. It was such a senseless attack, it broke Marim's heart. Kix was nothing next to the strong, bulky man. He was a minnow attacking a pike, a mouse trying to savage a dire.

Cockram swore again. He shook his head like a horse trying to dislodge a fly. Then his body went rigid. He screamed and his hands released their terrible grip. Marim felt Kix's swell of pleasure as he bit and clawed into the eye, his needle-like talons ripping and tearing, his teeth drawing forth pale fluid.

There was a dull slap: a hand smacking against skin. Then, there was pain. Overwhelming pain.

It wasn't Marim's pain this time. It was Kix's.

Cockram slapped his hand against his own face, Kix's tiny body caught between. The tessila's back snapped under the force of the blow.

Wings limp, Kix tumbled out of the air. Marim saw him fall. His body was a smudge of muted yellow on the gray air. He fell in a twist, turning wing over wing, to land like an autumn leaf in the dewy grass.

He lay there, forelegs clawing uselessly at the damp blades. His anger faded to confusion. He tried to right himself, tried to come to her.

He couldn't make it. His wings were too heavy, his legs too weak. He let out a thin, helpless cry.

Marim's tessila was dying.

She wanted to lie down next to him. She wanted to cup his delicate, broken body in her hands. She wanted to thank him for choosing her, for surviving all this time when some stronger, more spectacular tessila had given up. She wanted to apologize for never finding a way to heal him.

But Cockram's hands were on her throat again. They were damp now, warm and sticky with blood. *Good,* Marim thought. *I hope he loses that eye.*

She couldn't breathe. The gray blooms were back. Marim closed her eyes, ready to let go. Her mind wandered back to her years at the academy, the way all the other girls had spoken so fondly of their tessili. In the years after the kidnapping, Marim had always been a little embarrassed by Kix – his simple nature, his scarred hide. She tended to conceal him from the other girls, much as she concealed her scarred throat.

But, in the end, it was Kix who had fought for them, not Marim. As her ears began to pound again, Marim felt her heart swell with a new emotion. Kix was a tenuous spark at the edge of her consciousness now, but she pushed a thought towards him, along with an emotion she'd never felt before. Or, at least, hadn't felt since that terrible day Nylan had locked a collar around her throat. *I love you, Kix. Thank you. I love you.*

The world went black. There was an instant of nothing. Then the very earth seemed to split apart as a surge of magic rippled through the charged air.

There was a roar. Marim heard it even with her muffled ears.

Suddenly, Cockram's hands were gone. She could breathe again, barely. She gasped and choked. Her throat was raw, constricted, swollen. But she could breathe. She sucked in one glorious constricted breath, then another.

She heard the sound of a scuffle, muffled curses, running feet.

Then, all went quiet as Marim's world faded to black.

Vailria was running, careening down the path that sloped towards the warmlake, Embriem tramping behind her. The air flickered around her, but the roar she heard wasn't the growl of thunder. It was something else – a sound she'd never heard.

Tok was agitated. He was uncomfortable, for one thing. He'd been out of the water too long. He was scared as well, uncertain about the pulses of magic he could feel but not understand. He clung to her collar, chittering with anxiety. She could do little to sooth him. She didn't have any more answers than he did.

In the thick air ahead, Vailria saw a figure. She stopped, staring, as a man stumbled towards her. He hurried, limping, head down, hand clamped over one side of his face. When he noticed Vailria and Embriem, he froze in place for an instant. Then he left the path, melting into the fog as if he'd never been there at all.

Embriem caught up, coming to a stop beside her. "What is it? Why have we stopped?"

Vailria's heart was pounding. She stared into the fog. "Who was that?"

But Embriem hadn't seen, and there was no time. Vailria began to walk again. There was no more roaring, but the angry bellows had been replaced by a steady rumble that charged the restless air.

They walked on. The path was wet, water beginning to run in rivulets down the slope. Vailria's hair was heavy and chilled, her skirts sodden. She wanted nothing more than to be in her little house, lighting a fire and feeling Tok's quiet contentment as he swam in the warm water beneath the floorboards.

Up ahead, Vailria made out another shape in the fog. It was a second person, this one sitting on the trail. Nearby stood a strange creature. It was not terribly large – perhaps the size of a small hound. It had a long, sinuous body and neck, a sharp head. And wings.

Vailria stopped dead in her tracks. The rumble, she realized, was a low, angry growl. And she could make out another noise now: a thin, persistent cough.

Next to her, Embriem cursed quietly. "What in the name of Priam?"

Vailria began to move again. The fog was a restless screen between her and the two shapes. As she neared, the animal saw them and stepped in their direction, wings flared threateningly. The figure turned stiffly to look over her shoulder, spoke a few quiet words, and began to cough again.

It was Marim. There was no mistaking her. The creature next to her must be her tessila, grown to many times its normal size.

The animal was clearly incensed. Vailria could feel the rage boiling off him, curdling the misty air. His yellow scales were slick with damp, his eyes sharp and intelligent.

Vailria was so surprised, her thoughts stilled to nothing. It was Embriem who spoke. He'd stopped as well, hesitant to approach the massive, enraged tessila. "Marim," he called. "Where's Tassin?"

The girl made as if to answer, but her words were overcome by more coughing. She struggled to her feet, swaying, and set a hand on her tessila's scaled shoulder. She wobbled forward, unsteady as a newborn colt, her creature pressed close against her legs. As she approached, Vailria felt her heart constrict.

Something had happened to this girl. Her eyes were red-rimmed, her lips swollen. The collar of her blouse was askew and the dark smudges of bruises were beginning to form on the pale skin of her throat.

Vailria remembered the man, the one who had melted away into the fog. Her heart began to pound. What had happened?

Embriem took a step forward, his concern for his boy outweighing his fear of the overgrown tessila. "Marim." His voice was urgent. "My son. Where is he?"

Marim was close enough now Vailria could see blood vessels had burst in her eyes, making the whites dark and blotched. She shook her head, her expression lost. She croaked out a few words. "I don't know."

Embriem moved ahead, hurrying around her on the path. Vailria hesitated, not sure where she was needed most. She looked at Marim, but the girl waved a hand, indicating she should follow Embriem then turning to totter in that direction herself.

Together, the two women walked through the fog. They came upon Embriem a moment later. He was kneeling to one side of the path, a dark, flat outline of a man. They were close enough to the lake now Vailria could hear the sigh of the wind in the reeds, the gentle shush of the water. She felt a swell of longing, Tok's desire to go: to swim and climb and rest. But he would not leave her now, not when so much was unknown.

Embriem's shoulders were bowed. He heard them approach, and half turned. His face was streaked with tears. In front of him,

Vailria could see Tassin's crumpled form, his body arranged as if it had been dropped with no greater care than a bundle of reeds. He lay half on his back, face partway pressed against the damp grass, one arm out flung, the other folded beneath his body.

Again, Vailria thought of the man. She glanced at Marim, taking in the swollen lips, the bloodshot eyes, the bruised neck. Someone had tried to kill them, Marim and Tassin both.

Embriem's voice was choked and small. He knelt near his son, hands hovering as if he was afraid to touch the frail body. Then, gently, he adjusted Tassin so he lay on his back, arms tidy at his sides. "I think he's dead. He's not dead, is he?"

Vailria took a step towards them. That was when she noticed the brinlin.

There was a movement in the grass by her foot, so small she would not have noticed except Tok perked up with sharp interest. Her attention drawn, Vailria looked more closely. She saw the tiny creature struggling through the grass, hauling itself between the damp stems with its ill-suited webbed feet. It was orange with darker spots, blue, or purple maybe. She stared at it for a time, mystified. She'd never seen a brinlin leave the lake.

The grass next to the orange brinlin twitched. Vailria saw another, this one yellow with pale spots. Behind that came another, and another. There were dozens of them, all making their slow way from the lake towards Tassin.

"Embriem." Vailria spoke in a measured, steady tone, desperately aware now of his huge, clumsy feet in their thick-soled boots. Had he already crushed a brinlin, never seeing it in the fog?

It began to rain then – real rain rather than just soupy air. It hardly mattered; Vailria was already drenched through. "Embriem, I don't think he's dead. You mustn't move, though. The brinlins have felt him here. They're coming to him. They're all around you now. One among them might be the one who can save your son's life. If you move, you could crush her."

Embriem went very still. Marim, too, stiffened and began to stare down at the ground with a look of disbelief. She spoke, her words a hoarse croak. "They're everywhere."

They were everywhere. It seemed a hundred brinlins were gathering around Tassin. They were excited. One after the other, they released their light, mewling cries. Vailria felt a rush of awe, coupled with a small pang of guilt. No brinlin from this lake had bonded with a human in years.

In the grass, Tassin lay like a carcass. His skin was pale and slick in the rain. His hair was stuck to his forehead. Vailria couldn't make out any rise and fall of his chest. His eyes were closed. Surely, he still lived. Didn't he?

Marim was moving forward, picking her way one delicate step at a time towards Tassin. She reached the boy, knelt beside Embriem, and put a hand on the boy's forehead. "He's not dead." Her voice was a painful rasp that made Vailria wince. "Alive, but just."

Embriem surged to his feet, but remembered the brinlins. He stood rooted in place, swaying like a tree in a storm. "Do something. We must …"

"Embriem," Marim cut him off, her voice hoarse and wheezing. "Embriem, look down."

The man cut off midsentence. His body, alive with agitation, went still. He froze and fell silent, staring down at his foot.

A brinlin had crawled out of the grass. She perched on the humped leather of his boot's toe, delicate gills quivering in the rain. Her slick hide was pale blue, smattered over with silvery dots, luminous in the fog.

Rain ran into Vailria's eyes. She wiped it away. Slowly, as if in a trance, Embriem bent and offered the tiny creature his hand. The brinlin sniffed his fingers, flared her gills, and climbed into his palm. "Nel." Embriem spoke the word in a bemused tone, barely audible over the hissing rain and the sighing reeds. He looked at Marim, eyes wide with wonder. "Her name is Nel."

Marim was more than a little confused. First, there was her location. She was down by the warmlake, out in a downpour, wet to the skin. She had no idea how she'd ended up here. It seemed a moment ago she'd been in Embriem's house, trying to persuade him to leave the illusion of Tassin behind. Then, the next thing she knew, she was collapsed in the grass and Kix was all but overwhelmed with vicious anger.

Someone else had been there, at first – a looming figure in the fog. There'd been a scuffle and a shriek. Kix had come to her out of the wet air, scales shining, the size of a dog.

That fact alone had been surprise enough. In her years at the academy, Marim had spent countless hours trying to get Kix to shift. Every professor in the place had tried to help. They'd set up scenario after scenario, attempting to ignite different emotions, different desires. The theory had been that, since tessili healed themselves completely each time they changed size, whatever was wrong in Kix might be repaired if they could only get him to enlarge.

It had never worked. Marim had given up hope it ever would. Now, here in this sodden place, he stood before her with a wingspan as long as she was tall.

It was mind-bending, to say the least. But Kix wasn't the only mystery. Marim's body had taken a beating. Her throat felt raw and bruised. Her voice, when she tried to speak, was hoarse and choking. She had a persistent desire to cough. She had a vague memory of pressure – a vice on her throat. But that was all she could recall.

And there wasn't time to sort any of it out. Vailria and Embriem had appeared, asking questions she couldn't answer. Now, Tassin lay before her, pale and inert. His skin, when she touched it, was cold and waxy.

The boy needed help, and quickly. Marim closed her eyes, preparing a healing spell. Underneath her confusion and the pain of her throat, she was aware of a new sensation. It was an undercurrent in her mind, a dull roar in her psyche. She'd noticed it as soon as she'd come to on the ground, but she hadn't had a chance to try to figure out what it was.

Now, as Marim reached for her magic, she understood.

It was Kix. Or rather, it was the power Kix's existence allowed her to wield. Always before, his reserves had been shallow, the energy he offered a little listless.

Not so now. As Marim drew her focus down, she felt electrified with his energy.

It had worked as her professors had hoped. Kix had shifted, healing both himself and their bond.

She almost laughed with delight. So *this* is what it felt like. This was what casting was for everyone else. The sensation of all that power was electrifying. Marim had to resist the urge to seize at it in sheer, greedy, anticipation. Possibilities crowded into her mind, filling her with a desire to experiment. For a moment, she was overwhelmed with a giddy sense of triumph. *That's Kix,* she realized. *I'm feeling what he's feeling, and he's awfully proud of himself.*

Embriem said something. Marim was too caught up in her bond with Kix to make him out, but his voice pulled her back to the task at hand. *Later,* she promised her tessila. *A little later we'll have some fun, see what we can do.*

This thought seemed to please Kix. He settled in the grass, content to wait. Marim once again narrowed her focus down to the boy.

Tassin was alive, and he was surrounded by brinlins. They had formed a ring in the grass around him, dozens and dozens of the tiny creatures. She could feel them nudging at Tassin, sending out little probes of hopeful magic, trying to get him to latch onto one of them. But the boy was too weak. He was weak, he was unconscious, and his body was moments away from death.

He needed a boost. He needed a restoration of vitality. Fortunately, Marim had spent nearly her whole life studying the healing arts, and now she had Kix's new power to back her spells.

Marim set her hands on Tassin's forehead, one on either side. She drew in a long, slow breath, gathered her threads of magic, wove the spell, and released.

The surge of magic she sent into Tassin surprised even her. The boy snapped upright as if jerked by puppet strings. Vailria's voice snapped from nearby in the rain. "Be careful, boy. They're all around you."

Marim let her hands fall back to her sides. Tassin's hair was a sodden mop. Water ran in rivulets down his face. He was blinking and staring and quivering with shock. For a moment, his face was vague, his expression disoriented.

Then he looked down at a brinlin that had crawled onto his hand, and his face lit with a soft, ecstatic smile.

CHAPTER 7

The storm had moved on. Outside the drawing room windows, the sky was lit with a false dawn. The air was bright and fresh, the fog as thin as it ever got. Late light spilled into the room, drenching the furniture in rich afternoon tones.

It was several hours since they'd left the warmlake. Embriem had squelched back through the driving rain, dirty and soaked, never taking his eyes off his son. They'd encountered no one. When they'd reached the house at last, he'd been relieved to find it empty. There would be a reckoning with the rector later. So much to explain. But for now, all Embriem wanted was to see his son safe, clean, and dry.

And alive. Tassin was alive. He was not only alive, he was shining with vitality. He chattered the whole way back from the lake, rattling off question after question Embriem was unable to answer.

Embriem felt it too, a new undercurrent of life. Where the hunger had been before—a living, gnawing, drain—he now felt instead a vast well of energy. It was to do with Nel. He knew that much at least. As he walked, keeping an eye on Tassin, he cradled the brinlin's small, perfect body in his cupped hand.

They'd split up when they left the lakeshore. Embriem, Tassin and Marim heading for Embriem's house, Vailria promising to join them there once the storm passed. Tok, she'd explained, needed some time in the water.

Now, the sun was falling. Embriem had requested a large meal, which he and Tassin had eaten together, ignoring the startled looks of Secha and Baret. Now, the two of them sat in the drawing room, waiting for Marim and Vailria.

The latter arrived first. Embriem heard the distant sound of her knock. A moment later, the tall woman stepped into the drawing room. Down by the warmlake in her wet clothing, she'd had a wild, desperate look about her. Now, she was composed, dressed in her neat woolen dress. Her gray-shot hair was dry and tidy. Embriem understood the collar now. It allowed her brinlin to ride within, concealed and warmed against the skin of her throat.

As Vailria stepped into the room, Embriem turned with eager relief. His mind felt clear for the first time in days. He had so many questions. Was Tassin out of danger? Were he and his son like the Tessilari now, capable of wielding magics? How much time would their brinlin need to spend in the lake? Why did no one else on Cynnes Tarth know this could happen?

The questions swarmed in Embriem's mind, so many he couldn't get a single one out. Vailria proceeded forward. She crossed the great space, her soft shoes making no noise on the polished floor. As she neared, Embriem felt some of his happy anticipation fade. There was something in her expression that made him draw back a step.

She stopped a few paces away, glancing from Embriem to Tassin and back again. Tassin was seated on the floor, his brinlin perched on his finger. The tiny animal was stretched out in splendid contentment, absorbing the heat of Tassin's skin. Tassin was speaking to it in a low, excited stream of words. He'd been doing this ever since they'd left the dining room.

Embriem thought he understood. He felt a similar fascination with Nel, only his mind was too full of questions and ideas to focus on her in the same way. He gestured towards his son. "Is this normal?"

Vailria's steady gaze locked onto his. For a moment, Embriem almost remembered something. It was an old memory, dim with the passage of time. He seemed to be standing by the great forest, looking at Vailria, who was staring at him with her glittering eyes. He had just done something, something remarkable, something he was very proud of. He couldn't remember what, and Vailria was stepping forward, she was extending her hand.

She did the same thing now, speaking as she approached. "Embriem." There was a note of command in her voice. "We need to go."

Her hand settled onto his: a gentle touch. He felt an urge to pull back, to jerk away, but it faded as a soothing warmth seemed to flow into him. He had no reason not to trust Vailria. After all, she'd helped save his son's life.

"Go pack." The note of command was distinct now. "Bring only what you can easily carry."

The warmth bloomed past Embriem's hand, moving slowly through his body. He heard an angry chittering sound. Was that Nel? He wanted to turn his head, to look at his brinlin and see what she was upset about, but he couldn't look away from Vailria's eyes.

She was right, he realized with a dawning sense of certainty. He must pack. They must go.

He was on the verge of compliance. He would take his son and hurry to their rooms. He would give Tassin his old leather bag, he decided, and he himself would carry his trading pack. He was seconds away from internalizing Vailria's command when Marim burst into the room.

The girl's entrance was a shock, not the least because of her appearance. Where Vailria looked cool and composed, Marim was disheveled. Hair wild, the bruises on her throat standing out in stark contrast against her white skin, she flew into the room like an enraged banshee. Kix, small again, was an electric speck on the air. He flew straight towards Vailria and Embriem's joined hands.

"What are you doing?" Marim's voice was raw. She charged across the floor. She hadn't changed her clothing. Her dress was wet and there were creases on her face, as if she'd just woken from a deep sleep.

Kix, hissing, made as if to attack Vailria's hand. The woman snatched it back with a quick intake of breath.

The spell broke. There was a strange dip in Embriem's mind, like a bell ringing under water. The conviction he must pack, they must go, fizzled away and became nonsense.

Marim hurried forward, full of enraged energy. "What are you doing?" she said again. Her voice was shaking, full of rage. "You put me to sleep, somehow. You would have bewitched them into following you. You would have left me alone here if Kix hadn't managed to wake me up."

⫶

Marim's head felt muzzy with sleep. She was chilled from her wet dress. Her throat was so stiff and sore she could hardly swallow. She felt stale and disheveled and she was painfully aware of the contrast between her and Vailria as they stood facing each other in the drawing room.

Marim had no doubt she looked like a lunatic, but she was too shaken, too shocked, to care. Never in her life, in all her years at the academy, had anyone ever manipulated her with magic.

She could feel the residue of the spell clinging to her. It was sticky, hard to shake off. She remembered the walk home, following Embriem and his son through the downpour. When they'd parted ways with Vailria, the older woman had reached out, taking her hand and giving it a squeeze. They'd separated. Marim and Embriem and gone on. She'd grown more tired with every step, but that was hardly surprising, given all she'd been through.

Back at the house, she'd told Embriem she was going to wash up and change, but she'd barely managed to remove her sodden boots before collapsing onto the bed.

She'd woken later to the feeling of Kix's desperation. He was worrying her hand, nuzzling and pawing at it. He'd returned to his normal size when they left the lake, but she could feel the sense of urgency in him. She needed to wake up. She needed to go downstairs. Something was happening.

Now, facing Vailria, she wasn't sure she'd ever been so furious in her life. She felt foolish. Worse, she felt betrayed. Weren't they on the same side? Hadn't they worked together to save Embriem and Tassin?

Vailria said nothing. She faced Marim, seeming to weigh her with her gaze. Her brinlin was visible, peeping out from behind her collar, chattering with agitation. Marim felt her skin prickle with alarm. She tried to recall her old lessons at the academy, the ones she'd been so bad at. She drew up a passive shield spell and held it around herself and Embriem. It was possible Vailria would be able to punch through, but at least it would slow her down if she attacked.

Embriem looked confused. He was rubbing his head, eyes narrowed, looking from Marim to Vailria and back again. "Vailria? Can you explain?"

The woman's nostrils flared as if she was fighting to contain some intense emotion. "We have to go," she said. "The longer we stay, the more work I'll have to do to contain the damage."

Marim tried to speak, to ask the question. "What damage?" But her voice caught in her throat. She began to cough. A flash of irritation shot through her. With a giddy rush, she remembered the vast pool of new power Kix gave her access to. It was still there, even though he was small again. She pulled on impulse, wove in a hasty rush, and cast an active healing spell on herself.

She couldn't see her own transformation, but she could see the effect of it in the expressions on Embriem and Vailria's faces. She swallowed with relief as the throbbing pain in her neck and throat drained away to nothing. The tight feeling in her eyes dissipated. She invested heavily in the spell, and it did its work. A rush of warmth swept over her body. When it had passed, she felt energized and well.

But healing magic could only do so much. Her dress was sodden and clinging and filthy. She took a risk and cast an active ignition spell – one of the few bits of magic she'd been passingly good at back at the academy. She started the spell, targeting her entire dress, but stopped it before the fabric could get to the point of bursting into flame. A great billow of steam rose out of her skirts as the fabric went hot, then cooled. As the cloud dispersed into the room, Marim was, at least, mostly dry.

Rejuvenated, she turned to Vailria. "What damage?"

Vailria lifted her chin, eyes sparking with anger. She didn't answer. Instead, she turned to Embriem. "Embriem," she said, "you know me. You know you can trust me. There is more going on than I can summarize, but there is a long history here of violence against people like you, people like me. People like your son. I can take you to safety. It's what I'm here for. It's my roll."

Marim glanced at Embriem, afraid whatever history he had with Vailria would trump his new friendship with her. But he was shaking his head. "No." His tone was firm. "I'm not going anywhere until I understand what happened today. You can't expect me to walk away from my home, from my family?"

Vailria made a gesture towards Marim. "What do you think happened to her? What do you think nearly happened to your son? She didn't strangle herself. She didn't carry your son off and leave him for dead in the grass. Someone already knows what has happened. I must get you and Tassin safely hidden, figure out who attacked Marim, and fix this before it gets worse."

But Embriem was shaking his head. "Your argument is flawed, Vailria. Why should we hide? We've done nothing wrong. There is no law against taking a brinlin from the lake. There is no law against wielding magics. You can do what you like, but I'm going to stay. I'm going to stay and I'm not going to hide. If people here don't like what I've become, that's their problem. Not mine."

Marim felt a rush of satisfaction as Embriem spoke, but Vailria seemed to grow more angry with every word. Her reply was short and bitter. "You're a fool, Embriem. You have no idea what you're up against."

Some of the stiffness went out of the other woman, then. She looked suddenly gray and worn and tired. Marim felt a surge of empathy for her. Trying to ease the blow of Embriem's refusal to listen, Marim spoke. "There's no reason we can't all work together. If you explain, tell us what is happening, we can pool our resources and work for change."

Vailria drew herself up taller, her eyes glittering with anger. "No." The word was distinct. "Events have moved beyond my authority. I must go."

The woman turned and began towards the door. Marim felt a surge of relief. She let her shield fall.

The instant she did, she felt her mistake. There was magic on the other side of her magic, waiting to take hold. She felt it move over her, move through her, and fade away.

Marim and Embriem stood in the drawing room, looking at one another. She had the fading sensation someone else had been with them a moment before, but the idea was weak, and faded quickly.

She looked down at her dry but dirty dress and rubbed at her throat, half remembering a feeling of pain. But there was no pain now, and no one else in the room except for Tassin.

Disoriented, she turned for the door. "You and Tassin should rest," she said. "I'm going to go get changed."

Cockram tossed back another brandy. He sucked in his breath, gritting his teeth against the pain. His daughter had never been talented with a needle. Now she was as clumsy as she'd ever been, tugging and poking with unnecessary force as she attempted to sew the dangling flap of skin on his calf back into place. She worked in silence, head bowed over the wound, but Cockram could sense her skepticism. He'd told her he'd gone too close to the woods and been attacked by a dire. This was plausible in that the animals were known to sometimes hunt beyond the edge of the wood when the heavy storms set in. The bigger question, though, was what would have possessed Cockram to go to the edge of the wood at such a time.

Cockram couldn't worry about that now. The leg was painful, but it was nothing compared to the agony in his head. He didn't know what the tessila had done to his eye. Bitten it and clawed it, he thought. The pain had been immense, far worse than anything he'd ever felt before. He'd slapped the creature away and thought he'd killed it, but then it had come at him again, far larger than it had been before, a whir of fury and wings.

Letting go of Marim, Cockram had run to Tassin and scooped the boy into his arms. He'd heard the creature come crashing after him and run away, driven close to the warmlake even though that was the one direction he didn't want to go. He'd still been running when he felt teeth sink into his calf, vicious and tearing. With a shout of pain, Cockram tried to pull free, but the teeth were sunk too deep. In desperation, he threw the boy at the animal. There was a thud and a hiss and Cockram was able to tear free. Bleeding, mad with pain, he limped away, barely avoiding Embriem and Vailria when they'd appeared out of the fog. He'd pulled his rooster pin free of his scarf and stuck it through his lapel, wrapped the scarf around his leaking eye, and hobbled home.

Now he was enduring his daughter's clumsy ministrations. She'd replaced the scarf with a proper bandage, but not before he'd seen the fabric, soaked with blood and some sort of clear, runny liquid that made Cockram's guts loosen with disgust. He was worried. The leg would heal, but what about the eye?

At last, Tilde lifted her head, coiled the leftover gut and pushed back from his leg. His head was swimming with the drink and the pain. She seemed to waver and spin, becoming multiple images of herself as she walked to where the bandages were laid out on the bar.

She was back a moment later, wrapping his calf in a soft, clean batting. She was clumsy and slow, as usual, but at least she was taking care of him. That, Cockram reflected, was worth something.

As his thoughts drifted on a haze of liquor, Cockram had to admit he'd lost the round. If the boy had made it to the warmlake, he was one of them now: a monster, like Cockram's sister had been for a time. The girl, the Tessilar, complicated matters, but Cockram saw now he'd only lost because he hadn't been prepared.

He hadn't known Marim's creature could grow large that way. Now that he did know, he could factor that in, he could work it into his plan.

For a time, Cockram's thoughts slowed and shifted, becoming dreamlike. He remembered his sister, remembered the day she'd come running up the hill to their house, hands clasped gently before her. He'd been out in the side yard, shooting at squirrels with his old sling. She'd run up to him, face all flushed with excitement. She'd shown him what she held.

It was one of the little monsters from the lake. He could still see it, clear as day, with its bright hide and sharp eyes. He could still remember the feeling of revulsion that had crept through him, still remember her excited words. "Promise not to tell anyone? Promise?"

"There you go, Da." Tilde's rough voice brought him back to the present. His head felt huge with pain, his calf molten. He leaned in his chair, groping for the brandy bottle.

His daughter spoke again. "We'd best get you to bed. I'll need to open the place up soon. Lucky the storm kept everyone away."

Cockram grunted. She was right. They could not serve patrons with him passed out in a chair, bleeding into his bandages. "Help me."

His daughter did not protest. She waited as he heaved himself upright, bore his weight as he slung an arm about her shoulders and made his slow way across the reed strewn floor. The reeds were fresh, he noted. She must have put them out while he was gone.

As they fumbled up the staircase, Cockram cursing and staggering, his daughter supporting him, his mind strayed again to his sister. *Put this in her tea. Make sure no one sees you.* He remembered how the vitality had drained out of her, day by day. He remembered how she'd grown thin and listless. As he pushed through his bedroom door, he seemed to hear the death bell tolling.

If his sister had had to die, so too these others must die. It was a simple matter of how to bring it about.

Cockram made it to his bed. He was vaguely aware of his daughter adjusting the bedclothes, pulling the curtains, shutting the door.

This was fine. This was ok. Cockram had dealt with setbacks before. He would sleep for now. Tomorrow he would make a plan.

Embriem's back garden was a large space divided into sections by sculpted hedges, graveled pathways, and stone benches placed at strategic intervals. The weak morning sun filtered through the fog, giving the scene a soft appearance.

Marim and Embriem walked side by side. A sense of contentment resided between them, a feeling they'd accomplished something.

Tassin was asleep again. He had a long way to go on his journey back to health, but there was the bloom of life in his cheeks even when he slumbered. When he was awake, he was alive with excitement, full of verve and fascination. He'd already lost the skeletal appearance. His eyes were no longer bruised, his cheeks no longer sunken.

Embriem also radiated a certain vitality Marim hadn't seen in him before. As they walked together, he looked around as if seeing the world with new eyes.

Marim, too, felt as if everything had a special shine. Her renewed bond with Kix was still electrifying, the sense of her new potent power reassuring.

What was less reassuring was her memory. There were smudges in her mind, a muddling starting from the moment she returned to Embriem's house from her first visit to the warmlake and ending with standing in the drawing room before going upstairs to change. Trying to piece together what had happened in between was like looking at a charcoal drawing after a spray of water has splashed across the paper. Some parts were clear, others obliterated.

Embriem too, had only partial memories of what had happened between the house and the warmlake. His confusion was doubtless a side effect of the hunger. Hers was doubtless a side effect of over-extension. He was convinced it didn't matter. She wasn't so certain.

As they walked, Embriem spoke in a firm and steady tone, telling Marim his plan. "I won't hide." He'd said this several times already: to Marim, to his mother, to his son. "I won't hide what

I've become. Whatever happened in the past has no relevance in today's world. Masidon has accepted the Tessilari. Lan Dinas must learn to accept me and my son. You will help, Marim. You've been through this before, so you can share what you know, guide us through the difficulties. And you must teach Tassin. He must learn some spells." He paused, laughing. "My son will wield magics."

Marim thought of all the conflict she'd already seen in her short life. She thought of the brutal War of Diodsfall, the hundreds of fallen soldiers, the simmering resentment so many in Masidon still felt for her people. She thought of the dark looks, the harsh words that had so often been directed at her. She thought about the sailors, about what had happened on the ship.

It would not be easy. On this shiny morning, however, knowing this did not dampen her feeling of contentment. Part of it was coming from Kix. He'd gone through the stitchring last night and was currently gnawing his way through a brillbane husk after a full night of deep slumber. He was happy – as happy as she'd ever known him to be. Marim was aware of a new sensation in her own heart: her deep, abiding love for him.

Walking with Embriem, she couldn't seem to feel anything but optimism. Kix was healed at last. Marim, for the first time in her life, was needed. "What about you, Embriem? You will need to learn as well."

They turned a corner, walking along the edge of a shallow pond. Embriem waved his hand, batting away her comment like a buzzing a fly. He looked ahead and gave a little laugh. Marim tilted her head to look at him, an inquiring smile on her lips.

"That day, when I stopped you in the street, I thought you were the answer to a prayer. Then, for a short while, I thought instead I'd stumbled in some nightmare of a fairy story. But it turns out my first impression was correct."

Marim thought back. It seemed so long ago now she'd first stepped into Embriem's house, first laid eyes on his starving son.

As if following her train of thought, Embriem's smile faded. "Thank you," he said. "Thank you for helping me. I don't know how I'll ever repay you, but for now I hope you will continue to accept my hospitality. I hope you will stay."

As he spoke, Embriem reached out and took her hand. His fingers were much larger than hers, but his touch was gentle. Around the two of them, the fog was all aglow.

Marim knew nothing in life was this easy. She knew things would change. She knew she would again face adversity and pain.

For now, though, she was happy. She was appreciated.

She stopped walking and set her free hand on top of Embriem's. "Yes," she said. "Yes, I will stay."

Then she thought of the academy, of Coll's face as she rode away. She added to herself, *For now.*

Excerpt from

BRINLIN FOREST

Annals of the Brinlocks: Book II

A Story of Bydaira

Robin Stephen

Prelude

Marim stumbled down the hill, her sea bag heavy on her shoulder and her thoughts a wild scramble. Kix's emotions, intense but muddled, made her own blood boil with a directionless thirst for revenge. *Why is he so angry? Revenge for what?*

She had no time to sort it out, no time to try to understand. The sight of the ship drifting slowly away from the quay seemed to replay in her mind, the captain staring down from his place at the rail. He'd seen her, and it had made no difference.

She was stranded. But worse, according to Cockram, the mob she'd seen on her way up to the harbor was hunting *her*.

The smart thing to do would be to get out of Lan Dinas. She had her bag back now, her tablets, spellbook, food, extra clothing. She could go to the forest everyone was so afraid of. Kix could learn to hunt rabbits and small game. She could carve out an isolated life beneath the trees, at least until the simmering hatred in this place came down from a boil.

But Marim had a bad habit of not doing the smart thing.

Cockram was heading for Embriem's. The woman in the shifting cloak was following him. Marim was following the woman.

In the darkness, hurrying down the narrow track, Marim tried to make a complete list of facts – things she knew about her situation without a doubt. *I am stranded among people who believe I am an abomination.*

It was not a promising start to her list. Before she could get any further, Embriem's house came into view. Marim stopped short, arrested with the force of her surprise.

The mob was there, filling the space between the road and Embriem's stately mansion. Many carried torches. Others carried primitive weapons, like pitchforks and the strange, barbed hooks used to harvest reeds. She remembered the angry muttering she'd overheard, the dark energy that seemed to writhe and coil among these people, pushing them on. *There are so many of them,* she thought. *So many people who hate me.*

If these people were here on Embriem's doorstep, angry, looking for vengeance, it was because of Marim. She stood in the shadows on the other side of the road, quivering with uncertainty. If any one of these people saw her, that dark energy would take over. Would they kill her? Did they hate her so much as that?

She remembered the spark in Cockram's eyes, the way he'd tried to stop her on the road, Kix's sudden thirst for revenge. *Revenge for what?*

Marim's body seemed to remember what her mind could not. Her throat felt suddenly tight, her breathing growing shallow and laborious. She seemed to remember kneeling in the wet fog, listening to the sound of a scuffle. Kix's angry cry, a man's scream.

The thoughts faded. On the edge of the crowd, Marim saw the two figures she'd been following. The man, Cockram, had stopped to stare at the assembled group of people as well. The woman, with her carved staff and shifting cloak, stood behind him. Up on the road, she'd thought them enemies. Now, she noticed a certain similarity between them – the way they both stood with their weight on their heels, the lift of the chin, the set of the shoulders.

Even as she puzzled about this, the man suddenly surged to life. He spun on the woman, holding something small and silver in his hand. *Is that a stunrod?*

Black memories rose up from the depths of Marim's mind. She seemed to feel again the blank shock, the fuzzing pain that made her whole body seize into paralysis.

Before, Marim had been confused and scared, but also a little bit curious.

Now, she was terrified.

As she watched the man's quick, lashing blow, she saw the woman was not ready. She'd be hit, for sure, and she would fall just as Marim had fallen so often beneath the stunrod Nylan had used against her.

Who is this man? The fear had a sharp grip on her stomach now. *What have I overlooked about this place?*

Chapter 1

Braven lounged on a moss-covered boulder, strumming his lute and singing quietly to himself. All around, the forest was a massive, silent presence. The trunks of the great trees stood like stately pillars, their crowns lost in the dimming fog. The leaves were down this time of year, the branches bare and gray, but the ever-present ferns still brought a splash of green to the forest floor.

The moss was damp, of course. Everything in the forest was damp. This didn't matter to Braven. All of his clothing was resistant to the wet, kept fresh by a delicate drying spell woven into the fabric, and the fog was always warm. So he played in relative comfort, his fingers dancing over humming strings.

As it wouldn't do for cheerful lute music to be heard anywhere in the enchanted forest, Braven maintained a spell as he played his song. There wasn't a name for the spell. It was something he'd come up with on his own. He held it around himself so it distorted the notes of his light-hearted tune into the vague murmurings of spectral voices and the snarling growls of dires – the sorts of things the people of Lan Dinas would expect to hear if anyone gathered the courage to venture into the woods.

Keeping the forest creepy was Braven's job. He was good at it. He wasn't good at playing the lute, which was why he mostly did it out here where no one could hear.

He was nearing the end of the song when he felt the little buzz in his sternum that meant someone had crossed one of his perimeter lines. He stopped singing, cocking his head to listen while maintaining a quiet strum with his fingers. But he couldn't hear a thing.

Rising, Braven tucked his lute with his pack into the hollow at the base of the ancient tree behind him. Then he adjusted his cloak and strode off to see who'd tripped his alarm.

He didn't move with any particular urgency. In all his years working the woods, Braven could count on one hand the number of times he'd come across anyone other than a wary woodsman. He wasn't expecting anything untoward, so when the voices drifted back to him on the dim air, he froze with surprise.

The woodcutters who came into the forest were—as a rule—quiet, observant men who respected the trees and woods as a whole and had learned the trick of the massive misdirection spell that made the forest so easy to get lost in. They came in to gather deadfalls and dropped limbs, working quietly and efficiently, leaving as soon as their task was complete. Braven and his fellows did not harm these men, or even scare them too badly. They did die occasionally, but that was because the woods were dangerous even without Braven's help.

Woodcutters worked alone. The forest had a way of separating those who desired to remain together. So Braven was surprised when he heard not just the voice of one man, but several.

He drifted up behind a tree and pulled his cloak in tight about his body. He closed his eyes and focused, letting his sense of hearing swell and open until he could listen to the conversation of the men several yards away as clearly as if they stood right next to him.

"… knows we're in here," one of them was saying in a low, hesitant tone full of unhappiness.

The voice that answered was the opposite. It rang with confidence and bluster, the unmistakable bravado of some show-off trying to prove something.

"I tell you, it's all fairy stories. When was the last time someone actually died in this woods?"

"Tem Cutter nearly died." These words were spoken by a third voice, short and surly.

There was a thump, as if someone had set a heavy burden down with impatience. "Tem Cutter. Tem Cutter! Why is it he's all anyone ever talks about? Yes, so a snake bit him. He stayed all night beneath the trees. He beat off a pack of dires with his bare hands. If that proves anything, it's that we're all behaving like imbeciles when it comes to this place."

Braven felt his normally sunny mood darken a few notches. He sidled around the tree, straining into the fog, but he could see nothing.

There was no response from the boastful man's companions. Braven considered his options. He had any number of old standby spells he used to spook the woodcutters if they grew too bold. This situation was different, though. These men were here to challenge the forest's mystique. That couldn't be tolerated. He might need to come up with something a little more creative.

"Anyway," the man began again, his voice ringing with hubris. "I've had enough of scraping and scrounging and breaking my back for a pittance. I've had enough of sitting on my hands while there's a fortune in fine timber sitting here for the taking. You two stand back."

Braven felt a prickle at the back of his neck – a warning pulse that something was about to happen. He felt a brief longing for Gia's presence. She was back at the lake. He rarely brought her on his patrol. It was too cool in the forest for her, and she grew uncomfortable out of the water. The bond between them was muted now, made thin by the distance.

A strange sense of urgency making him less cautious than usual, Braven hurried forward, moving on soft feet over the loamy forest floor. He stepped around a final tree just as he heard a loud, sharp, smack and saw a burly, middle-aged man standing with feet planted, shoulders braced, the head of his axe buried up to the shaft in the trunk of one of the sacred trees.

Braven was so shocked, so sickened by the sight, for a moment he could only stare. The man began to work his shoulders, prying the axe head loose. Then he heaved it back again, preparing for another swing.

Rage erupted in Braven in a sudden violent burst. The world seemed to waver as his vision went red at the edges. He felt heat rise to his face. His brain filled with an unfamiliar desire.

He wanted to harm these men.

The man with the axe grunted, reset, and swung again. Again, that horrible sound, the crack of metal biting ancient bark. The man laughed. "See." His voice had a gloating tone. "It's just a blighted tree."

Braven could see the other two men now. They stood a little distance off, shifting uneasily and casting glances into the fog. Though they were only a few trunks past the place where the forest gave way to grass, one of them held a string that stretched back to the wood's edge. They must have tied it off on their way in, so they could find their way back out.

The first man was still talking. "We're going to make our fortune, lads." He pulled the axe free and reset for another strike. It seemed to Braven he was not very handy with the tool. He'd seen other woodcutters chopping their way through deadfalls. They swung with clean, efficient strokes. This man was clumsy.

The thought gave Braven an idea. His rage was a living thing inside him now. He gathered his power, holding it in his mind and bringing it to a focus. Then, he waited.

Everyone always said Braven was talented when it came to casting. He supposed it was because most of what he did was intuitive. He had a feel for the power Gia lent him, and an innate understanding of what could be done with it. While nothing he did felt particularly remarkable to him, many of his peers had to learn their casting spell by painstaking spell.

Braven didn't think. He simply did. The axe rose for a third strike, and Braven sent out thread of magic on a moving pulse. He watched with grim satisfaction as the muscles beneath the man's shirt flexed. The axe began to fall, its head glinting in the dull light.

The scene seemed to blur. There was a thud, but this time the sound was not as crisp. It was the smack of metal striking flesh rather than bark.

There was a single beat of silence before the man began to scream.

✝

Marim still wasn't easy about the fog. As she reached the end of the garden walk and crossed the gravel yard to the back entrance of Embriem's large house, it annoyed her she couldn't see into the distance. Six months here, and she'd learned the different types of fog, when it was likely to be thick, thin, or restless. She'd made it through the violent storms that came with the changing seasons. The systems swept across the island and lingered, battering Embriem's house for two or three days sometimes.

After the storms moved on, she'd watched the angle of the light change. As the nights grew slightly cooler and shorter, some trees lost their leaves. Others did not. The hedges and grasses were still green, and there was never any frost or snow. Marim found this strange. It would be the dead of winter in Masidon now, the land frozen and dormant, waiting for spring.

The false winter lent a sort of dreamlike quality to Marim's sense of the passage of time. She felt she had been in this place for ages, and also that she had only just arrived.

And always, there was the fog. It muffled the world every time she set foot outside, making her feel as if she'd lost some sixth sense she'd never previously appreciated.

As she walked, Marim was aware of Kix wheeling above in the damp air. He came to her as she stepped onto the stone stoop and over the threshold, burrowing his small body between her hood and the skin of her throat. She gave a small, gasping laugh. "Kix, you're cold." But she said it fondly, reaching up to run a quick, affectionate finger down his sinuous back.

Her tessila found a comfortable position against her collarbone, and fell still. Marim closed the heavy double doors behind her. They had a tendency to boom if swung quickly, so she guided them shut before turning to make her way up the long hallway that led to the front of the house.

She was about to turn into the entryway and head for the stairs when she heard a door slam. Startled, she turned in time to see Embriem come striding out of his office, holding a letter in his hand. His red tinged hair was sticking out in every direction, his expression dark.

"Baret!" He thundered his butler's name, then noticed Marim standing at the mouth of the hall. Some of the annoyance smoothed out of his face. He modulated his tone, inclining his head in greeting. "Marim. Good day. I didn't see you there. Where's Tassin?"

It was strange, Marim thought, you could live in the same house with a man and see so little of him. Until this moment, she hadn't so much as clapped eyes on Embriem in days. Now, she couldn't help but note certain details about his appearance. He was pale, for one thing, even more so than was normal for the people here. He was still too thin. Unlike his son, Tassin, who had wasted no time packing back on the weight he'd lost during his ordeal, Embriem was not exhibiting much of an appetite. More alarming than all that, though, was the strange, restless glitter in his eyes.

Marim turned to face her employer, resisting the urge to reach up and confirm her collar was high and snug about her throat. "He's with Secha, having his lunch. Mishi will have him changed in time for his piano lesson."

The glitter in Embriem's eyes sparked. Some of the anger came back into his face. He held up the letter and spoke in a disgusted tone. "It would seem Master Flagron no longer cares to be in my employ."

Marim felt a dip of anxiety in her stomach as she stared at the innocuous piece of parchment. She groped for some mollifying statement, some way to put a spin on this latest snub, but her mind was a blank.

Embriem waited, standing next to an oil painting of a ship on the sea in a gilded, ornate frame. His finely made but somewhat rumpled clothing hung loose around the sharp angles of his body. She almost didn't believe her memory of the first time she'd seen him. He'd been so hearty and solid, striding out of the fog with the confidence of a man who is secure in his own place.

When Marim didn't speak, Embriem's shoulders sagged. His eyes drifted to the misty view out the window. "Just as well." His voice was low now, and tired. "His rates are astronomical."

Marim's eyes flickered around the ornate hall. It was dim, even at this peak hour of the day. When she'd first arrived in this house, lamps had been lit in the main living areas all of the time.

Not anymore.

It wasn't any of Marim's business, of course, but it was difficult not to hear the rumors. Though Marim did not go to town often (and when she did, the locals looked at her askance) she overheard gossip nonetheless. Now that Marim was a long-term occupant, Embriem had expanded the household staff by bringing on a live-in housemaid, a nurse to attend Tassin when he wasn't with Marim, and a footman. More than once, Marim had overheard quiet conversations in the back halls. The talk on the island was Embriem's business was struggling.

Marim was grateful to Embriem, but she also knew her own security and stability depended on his. When she'd had nowhere to go, no way to earn her keep, he'd given her a job. Marim was now Tassin's governess. In exchange for teaching his son reading, writing, arithmetic, and basic magics, Embriem provided her food and board, plus a weekly stipend.

It wasn't an outcome Marim had ever expected when she'd first set foot on the deck of the ship that had brought her here. But then, she'd never expected to be dumped off on this strange island either. For the most part, she was grateful to have a roof over her head. Tassin was a sweet child, if a bit disinclined to focus on the non-magical aspects of his education. If Embriem was nothing more in her life than a polite, distant presence, she could hardly complain.

Still, she was concerned for him. She'd learned a lot about the brinlins and their needs since taking over Tassin's care. She couldn't help but prod. "Embriem, when was the last time you went down to the warmlake?"

Embriem stirred, his eyes flicking to her only to slide off again. "Nel's there now." Before she could point out he hadn't answered her question, he seemed to rouse himself. "I'm sorry, Marim. Please excuse me." He strode off towards the back door, once again calling for his butler.

Marim stood looking after him. That would explain the strange glitter in his eyes. She lifted her hand to her neck and ran a finger along Kix's back again. The warmlake was at least two miles away. She and Kix had never been separated by such a distance in all the years since he'd chosen her as his partner. "He's running himself ragged." Marim murmured these words to her tessila as she continued her interrupted journey, up the staircase, down the broad hall, and into her own room. Inside, she closed the door and hung her damp cloak on one of the hooks on the wall.

As was her habit, Marim went first to her desk and removed a slim wooden case from the top drawer. She undid the clasp, feeling the spark of magic in her fingertips as the spell within confirmed her identity. She opened the lid and tipped out the three leather tablets within. They were all identical in size and shape. Two of them had seals stamped into the corner. The first bore the crest of Tessili Academy. The second, Professor Liam's personal chop. The third had no identifying mark.

Marim settled herself into her chair and spread the tablets out in front of her. Two of them, the two with the seals, bore writing. The third did not. As Kix darted off towards the fireplace, Marim read. She took in the words line by line, first from one tablet, then the other. She had picked up her scribis to begin a reply when she noticed something unusual.

The third tablet, the one that bore no seal, suddenly began to change. Words appeared, letter by letter, as someone far away wrote on the tablet linked to this one.

Marim turned from her writing, heart beginning to beat a little faster at the sight of the familiar, slanted hand. She read the words as they formed. "Does Kix socialize with the brinlin?"

This was typical of the tablet's owner. No small talk, no pleasantries, just opaque questions.

Nevertheless, Marim couldn't help herself. She pushed the two other tablets aside and began her answer.

KEEP READING
http://robinstephen.com/brinlinforest

FREE GIFT

Thank you for reading *Brinlin Isle,* the first installment in *Annals of the Brinlocks.* If you enjoyed the book, you might like to join Robin Stephen's mailing list. You'll get some exclusive Bydaira content for free, just for signing up.

To learn more, visit robinstephen.com/free

BOOKS BY ROBIN STEPHEN

Chronicles of the Tessilari
Tessili Academy
Tessili Rogue
Tessili Revenge

Annals of the Brinlocks
Brinlin Isle
Brinlin Forest
Brinlin Cove